Praise for *A F*

"My favourite of Cameron's
original premise, captivating plo
It's also a timely and urgent reminder of the power or the ...
the beauty of difference, and the importance of protecting everyone's
stories from those who seek to silence and erase us."
Simon James Green, author of *Boy Like Me*

"Sophie Cameron pushes the boundaries between reality and fantasy
in this warm, relatable, page-turning story, full of sparky ideas and perfectly
capturing the joys and awkwardness of teenage friendships."
Sarah Hagger-Holt, author of *The Fights That Make Us*

"I'm completely in awe of Sophie Cameron's ability to find new, original lenses
through which to view being human. This is another fun and compelling story
about the joys and perils of growing up. It's fantasy made real and relatable."
Nicola Penfold, author of *Where the World Turns Wild*

"A seamless blend of realism and the fantastical, written with Cameron's
signature wit, heart, and care, with an eye on the big questions: how do
friendships work? What's so important about imagination? Why are bookshops
so vital? And, of course: is the Loch Ness Monster actually really real?"
Sinéad O'Hart, author of *The Time Tider*

"A wonderfully inventive story about the importance of imagination
and the value of very real friendship. A lovely story about how we can
all imagine the reality we want and then work hard to make it real."
Anna Zoe Quirke, author of *Something to be Proud Of*

"Beautifully written and near impossible to put down …
a love letter to storytelling in all forms."
Netgalley review

"Full of fun, this is a lovely, inclusive read … a story about relationships,
not making assumptions about others and overcoming fear of failure."
Netgalley review

"A great book showcasing creativity, imagination and the love of literacy."
Netgalley review

For Grace – thank you for always being my first (and fastest) reader!

LITTLE TIGER
An imprint of Little Tiger Press Limited
1 Coda Studios, 189 Munster Road,
London SW6 6AW
www.littletiger.co.uk

Imported into the EEA by Penguin Random House Ireland, Morrison Chambers,
32 Nassau Street, Dublin D02 YH68
www.littletigerpress.com

A paperback original

First published in Great Britain in 2025
Text copyright © Sophie Cameron, 2025
Cover copyright © Helder Oliveira, 2025

ISBN: 978-1-78895-736-6
e-ISBN: 978-1-78895-776-2

Printed and bound in the UK.
STP/3400/0633/0225

MIX
Paper | Supporting
responsible forestry
FSC® C013604

The Forest Stewardship Council® (FSC®) is a global, not-for-profit organization dedicated to the promotion of responsible forest management worldwide. FSC® defines standards based on agreed principles for responsible forest stewardship that are supported by environmental, social, and economic stakeholders. To learn more, visit www.fsc.org

10 9 8 7 6 5 4 3 2 1

A FLASH OF NEON

SOPHIE CAMERON

LITTLE TIGER
LONDON

One

Bookshops are full of stories, and not just on the pages. The customers tell them too. Sometimes, when I'm helping out in my mums' shop, I people-watch and get ideas for the novel I want to write one day. I'll see two strangers sneaking looks at each other over the cookbooks and imagine they're having their meet-cute moment while I rearrange the shelves. Someone will rush in, red-faced and out of breath, and I'll pretend they're a diamond thief who's decided to hide from the police in our children's section. I've always liked the idea of being part of some big, dramatic scene – even if it is as an unnamed face in the background – of playing a role in someone else's adventure.

But today my own big story begins.

Today is the day my best friend Neon is due to visit.

I sit behind the till and scroll through his profile on my phone while Mum sorts out a delivery of new books. Dozens of photos glide past: Neon's smiling, freckled face; his beloved dog, Cauliflower; books he's read and songs he's addicted to. The most recent posts are all from his trip to the UK. Last week, he and his mum flew from their home in New York City to London, where his uncle lives.

His page is currently full of photos of tourist spots like Buckingham Palace and Big Ben, plus photos of his uncle's cat and the squirrels in Hyde Park. (Neon loves animals — it's one of the things we have in common. I can't have a dog because one of my mums is allergic, but if I could I'd have a bichon frisé like Cauliflower.)

"Laurie?" Mum dumps a stack of hardbacks on to the counter. "How about you actually earn the money we're paying you instead of staring at your phone all day?"

I glance up from the screen. My mums' bookshop is called Every Book & Cranny, and for the past year I've been helping out here for a few hours at the weekend. As well as the people-watching opportunities, I love organising the window displays and writing recommendation cards after I've read a good book.

But today I'm too nervous to think about anything except Neon's arrival. After London, he'd planned a couple of days in Edinburgh with his mum before travelling up north on his own to see me. His train is due to arrive in Inverness about an hour from now. I try to imagine it: his dark curls bouncing as he steps on to the platform, the way he might tug on the straps of the purple backpack that he takes everywhere as he scans the station.

I still can't really picture it. Neon is like his name, loud and bright and colourful. He'd stand out a mile in my small Scottish town.

"Sorry." I put my phone down on the counter. Mum is still glowering at me, so I spin round and tuck it behind the vase of flowers on the windowsill. "I'm back to being employee of the month now. Promise."

My older brother Joel pokes his head out from behind

the non-fiction shelves. "Uh, excuse me. *I'm* employee of the month."

"We've never picked an employee of the month, but if we did it would obviously be Gio," Mum says, which is true – Gio is the bookshop manager, and the entire place would probably fall to pieces if he wasn't there to run the show. "I'm counting on you two to help out while we're away this week, though. Especially on Gio's days off."

Joel moves his hand up and down to gesture at his body. "Hello? I came all the way from St Andrews to do exactly that, even though I have about a million essays to write. But have I had a thank you from Mutti? One single *danke schön*? No."

Mutti, our other mum, is an author. She has a new book coming out on Thursday, and tonight she's flying down to London for a whole week of interviews and events. Usually she goes alone, but this time Mum is tagging along. She claims it's to network and provide moral support, but I think she secretly wants a break to wander round galleries and drink overpriced coffee. Joel has come home from university for the week to help Gio out and make sure I don't burn the house down, or whatever it is my parents think I'd do if I was left alone for a week.

That's why I thought this would be the perfect time for Neon to visit. My mums are pretty relaxed, but I haven't told them anything about our friendship. They wouldn't understand.

"You're a saint and a martyr, Joel." Mum ruffles his dark brown hair. "Just don't leave the door unlocked again and we'll be fine."

As Joel protests that he only did that *one* time, the bell

7

on the door tinkles and Mutti shuffles in wearing her favourite fuzzy red cardigan and holding a cup of coffee. 'Mutti' is the German word for 'Mum'. Joel and I call her that because she's originally from Munich, though she's lived in Scotland for so long that she's almost completely lost her accent.

"Morning," she says, yawning. "Is it still morning?"

"It's almost midday, so just." Mum smiles but her words are clipped around the edges. "What time did you go to bed?"

"Three, I think? I fell asleep in the middle of editing." Mutti edges on to the seat beside me and hugs me with her free arm. Her eyes light up at the stack of hardbacks on the counter. "Ooh, is that the new Ruth Ozeki? I didn't think we'd get it in until next week."

While she and Mum are distracted, I slip out from behind the counter with my phone, curl up in the cosy armchair in the children's section and open Neon's profile again. Our most recent comments to each other are below a video uploaded this morning, a short compilation of tourist spots around Edinburgh. *New favorite city*, the caption reads. (*Nah, second favorite. Nothing beats NYC.*) *Now heading north to go see Laurie!*

I replied a few minutes after it was posted: *So so SO excited!* followed by a dozen of the yellow hearts I use only for Neon. His response was a line of purple ones, the colour he saves for me. I wonder how many purple and yellow hearts have been sent between our accounts in the past six months. Probably millions. Usually my phone doesn't go more than an hour without lighting up with a notification, apart from the seven or eight hours when the East Coast is asleep.

But since that photo there's been nothing. No new posts, no messages to me. Anyone looking at his profile could tell that's not like Neon. I bite the corner of my nail and refresh the page, as if that might make something pop up. Still nothing.

The bell on the door tinkles again. Mum looks up hopefully – we've only had a handful of customers since we opened two hours ago, and one was just looking for a bathroom. Her shoulders sink slightly when she sees who's arrived.

"Hi, girls. Laurie? Caitlin and Hannah are here."

My heart instantly drops at the sound of my friends' names. I stand up, the phone almost slipping from my hands, and hurry out from behind the shelves. Caitlin and Hannah are wearing matching denim jackets and they both have their hair up in high ponytails. They beam at me and Caitlin bounces on the balls of her feet.

"Today's the big day!" she says in a sing-song voice. "Are you excited?"

I widen my eyes to tell her to be quiet, then quickly usher her and Hannah outside, letting the door slam behind us. It's a cold Saturday morning in October, with only a few people wandering down the high street. The shop windows are thin, and Joel is nosy, so I drag Caitlin and Hannah away from the door and towards the Co-op.

"My parents don't know about Neon, remember?" I hiss.

"Oh, sorry, I forgot!" Caitlin clamps a hand to her forehead, but her smile still stretches right across her face. "I'm just excited for you! Are you nervous?"

"Yeah," I say, pushing my hair behind my ears. "I mean, a bit."

"Don't you need to leave for the station soon?" Hannah checks the time on her phone. "His train is due in at around one thirty, right?"

I didn't tell her or Caitlin that. They must have looked up the timetables, worked it out from the post on Neon's account this morning. "Um, yeah, I think so. But I told Neon how to get here, what bus he needs to take…"

Caitlin looks scandalised. "Laurie, no! This is your big romantic reunion – you *have* to meet him off the train."

My cheeks instantly go red. As I've told them a hundred times, there's nothing romantic between me and Neon. "It's not like that. He's my friend."

"Sure. If you say so." Caitlin tries to wink at me, but it looks like she's got a lash in her eye. "Don't worry – we'll come with you."

"No, you don't have to…"

"But we want to!" She crosses her arms, her expression suddenly serious. "Plus it's safer. Isn't that the number-one rule of meeting someone off the internet? You don't go alone."

"Neon isn't exactly *off the internet*," I say.

That's another thing I've told Hannah and Caitlin multiple times – that Neon and I met in Brighton last summer, while he was on holiday and I was visiting some family friends with my mums.

"Still, better safe than sorry," Hannah says. "I want to go to the shops anyway. I need some new mascara."

"Let's go, then. There's a bus in ten minutes." Caitlin peers past me and towards the bookshop. "Or maybe we could ask Joel for a lift?"

"No!"

The word is almost a shriek, but Caitlin's smile doesn't fade. A sickly feeling creeps into my stomach. Going to the station to pick Neon up with them is honestly the *last* thing I want to do, but I know Caitlin, and I know she's not going to back down now.

"Fine, we'll take the bus," I mutter. "I just need to get my money."

I trudge back to Every Book & Cranny, leaving Caitlin and Hannah outside – I can already sense the way they're grinning at each other behind my back. Inside the shop, Joel and Mutti are rearranging the fiction table to make room for the new arrivals while Mum is frowning at the computer by the till.

"What was all that about?" Joel asks, raising his eyebrows. "What did Caitlin mean by the big day?"

"Um, Lewis Capaldi has a new single coming out. She's a big fan." Joel thinks he's above listening to anything that makes it on to the charts, so I know that'll put an end to his questions. I lean on the counter and turn to Mum. "Is it all right if I go into town? And can I have my pay for this week now, please?"

Her face falls. "Your shift isn't over for another hour, Laurie."

Mutti waves a hand at Mum to say it's fine. "Let her go, Liv. It's quiet anyway."

"She needs to learn some responsibility!" Mum's expression turns stormy. "She won't be able to wander off whenever she likes when she has a real job."

"She's fourteen. She's got plenty of time to learn."

Mutti takes her wallet from her cardigan pocket and pulls out a couple of notes. Mum throws her hands up and disappears into the storeroom, muttering something about "never listens" that could be about me or Mutti, or maybe both of us. I catch Joel's eye, and he pulls a face. Our parents have been snapping at each other a lot lately. Whether we're at home or in the shop, the atmosphere often feels like it's about to shatter under a weight I don't quite understand.

"It doesn't matter," I say, trying to smooth over the tension. "I'll stay and finish the shift. Caitlin and Hannah won't mind."

"No, it's fine. Go." Mutti hands me the money with a tight smile. "But be back at five so we can say goodbye before our flight, OK?"

I pocket the notes with a thank you, then shout bye to Mum and Joel and head outside. Caitlin and Hannah are waiting on the doorstep, both grinning widely. The nervous feeling in my stomach expands into full-blown nausea, and I mentally kick myself for ever telling them about Neon's visit. This is one turn I did not want my story to take.

Two

The town where we live is a small, sleepy place on the banks of Loch Ness. The bus to Inverness only comes by once an hour and it's often late or early, and sometimes doesn't turn up at all. As Caitlin, Hannah and I hurry down the high street, I keep my fingers crossed that we've missed it, but unfortunately it's waiting patiently outside the fish-and-chip shop when we get to the stop.

I buy a return ticket with the money that Mutti gave me and reluctantly follow my friends upstairs. There's a parent with a toddler pretending to drive by the front window and a couple of older people dozing a few rows behind. Caitlin and Hannah sprawl out across the back seat, so I take the one in front and twist round to look at them.

"You *really* don't have to come to the train station with me. You can do your own thing and I'll meet up with you later."

"We told you, it's totally fine." Caitlin starts pulling her long dark hair into one of those messy buns that she does so well. "It's not every day your best friend comes to visit."

"American internet best friend," Hannah clarifies. "We're your real-life besties obviously."

Caitlin, Hannah and I have been friends since our first day of high school, when we all cracked up laughing at Caitlin's terrible attempt to draw a horse in Art. If our school was set up like a teen movie, they'd be the Popular Girls – they're both super pretty, and they both have older sisters who have shown them how to do their eyebrows and paint their nails. I'm not like that. My hair is dull and mousy, and my mums won't let me get it dyed until I'm sixteen. There are always spots on my cheeks and forehead, and no matter what I wear it never quite seems to fit right. Even after two years, I still can't really believe they want to be friends with me.

"Are you going to kiss him when you see him?" Hannah asks, cupping her face in her hands.

There's a kick of nerves in the bottom of my stomach. "I told you, it's not like that."

"Sure, sure." Caitlin grins. "I bet you're *dying* to kiss him again."

"You should do a slow-motion run across the station towards each other." Hannah makes a dramatic pumping motion with her arms. "It'd be so romantic."

Caitlin giggles. "Maybe he'll pick you up and carry you out, like in that film – the one with the guy in the white navy uniform, you know?"

They both start singing some cheesy ballad (Caitlin and Hannah go to musical-theatre classes together and are always bursting into song) but then a fourth-year boy who Hannah thinks is cute gets on the bus and distracts them. I mumble something about feeling sick, then turn round and stare out of the window as the bus lurches away from the pavement and down the high street.

Between the chippie and my parents' bookshop are several empty plots with To Let signs and boarded-up windows. Until last year, our little town attracted lots of tourists, but since the boats that sail down Loch Ness stopped coming here, the number of people visiting has dropped massively. Add that to the pandemic and we've lost two cafés, the newsagent, a toyshop and a jeweller. I know my mums are worried that Every Book & Cranny might be next.

But I don't want to think about that. The journey into Inverness takes twenty minutes and I spend most of them trying to come up with an excuse to stop Caitlin and Hannah from following me to the train station. When we get off the bus, I suggest that they wait in a café while I go and meet Neon.

"It might be a bit overwhelming for him, having all three of us there," I explain. "He's quite shy, so…"

Caitlin checks for traffic before striding across the road to the train station. "He doesn't sound shy. Not from what you've told us about him."

"We'll stand way back by the doors," Hannah says. "You won't even notice we're there."

"But I'm not sure he's even coming!" My eyes are starting to sting, and my voice is getting higher and higher. I come to a halt outside the station entrance. "Look, the truth is I – I haven't heard from him since he got on the train this morning. That's not like him. Maybe something happened. Some emergency."

"Like what?" Caitlin shrugs. "He's probably got no signal. It's always patchy on the train."

Hannah is starting to look uncomfortable. "How about

we…" she says, but Caitlin clicks her tongue, a sign that she's losing patience.

"Oh, come on. We're here now, aren't we? Let's *go*."

She links her arm through mine and marches me into the station. A small crowd of people wait by the ticket barriers, checking their phones or gazing at the platforms. When I turn round to look at the departures board, praying for a delay – anything to give me a few more minutes to get Caitlin and Hannah out of here – a voice over the loudspeaker announces the arrival of the 13:34 service from Edinburgh Waverley. My stomach drops as a long train edges round the bend in the rails and approaches platform 2.

"Here we go!" Caitlin says, drumming her fingers on my arm. "The moment of truth."

In a chorus of squeaks and wheezes, the train slowly rolls to the end of the track and comes to a stop. The doors slide open and people pour on to the platform: weary-looking parents dragging little kids and suitcases, students with backpacks and headphones in their ears, a large flock of older ladies chattering and rummaging in their handbags for their tickets. Caitlin stands on her tiptoes to try to spot Neon. After a few minutes, the torrent of travellers trickles down to a stream, but there's no sign of a curly-haired boy with freckles and a birthmark above his eyebrow.

"I guess…" My mouth has gone dry and my hands are clammy. I take out my phone to check for notifications, though I already know there won't be any. "I guess he's not coming?"

"Maybe he got on the wrong train," Caitlin says. "Why don't you call him and ask?"

Hannah bites her lip. "Let's just go to the shops or something. He'll send you a message if he does turn up."

"What do you mean *if*? Of course Neon's going to turn up." Caitlin looks at me. I can feel my cheeks getting redder and redder. "He *is* going to turn up, isn't he, Laurie?"

She smiles the way a tiger might smile before it pounces on its prey. The sickly feeling spreads, travelling up my gut and into my throat. Here's the thing: Caitlin and Hannah don't believe Neon exists. I see the way they smirk at each other before they ask a question about him, the laughter in their voices every time they say his name. I don't know why they came here today, but I know they never, not for a single second, expected him to actually get off the train. Maybe they wanted to find out what I would say when he didn't, how I'd explain or excuse it. Maybe they wanted to embarrass me.

I open my mouth – whether to answer Caitlin or vomit all over the floor, I don't know. Before I can do either, a voice shouts out across the train station.

"Laurie!"

We all spin round. There's a boy running down the platform towards us, arms waving above his head, a purple rucksack bouncing against his back. He has curly brown hair, deep brown eyes in a freckly oval face and a birthmark shaped like France above his eyebrow. The sight of him is such a shock, I have to grip the ticket barrier for balance.

"N-Neon?" I whisper.

"Sorry! Couldn't find my ticket." He sounds exactly as I'd imagined with a New York accent just like in the movies. "I can't believe I'm actually here! This is wild."

He slips his ticket into the machine, and the barrier

opens to let him through. For a long moment, we all stare at him. He's wearing a *Star Wars* T-shirt that I always see advertised online and the pair of sustainably made trainers that I keep asking my parents for. Behind the freckles, his face is slightly pink from running.

"I didn't think—" Caitlin looks as stunned as I feel. "We didn't think – we thought you were—"

"Are you OK, Laurie?" Hannah puts her arm round me, then smiles at Neon. "I think she's actually speechless."

I can't even nod in response. This is unbelievable. And I don't mean that it's surprising or astonishing or any of the other ways that people use that word – I mean this is actually *impossible to believe*. I don't know whether I'm hallucinating, or trapped in a dream, or have been duped into appearing on one of those prank TV shows, but Neon Hart cannot be standing in front of me. He just can't. It can't be true.

Because Caitlin and Hannah were right: Neon doesn't exist.

I made him up.

Three

Neon Hart is the same age as me, but he was born six months ago. It was a Friday in April, bright and surprisingly warm for spring. Caitlin, Hannah and I had bought sandwiches from the Co-op for lunch and taken them to the park instead of eating in the canteen. They had a show coming up for their musical-theatre class, so after we'd eaten they practised a dance routine while I sat on the grass and made daisy chains.

Sometimes I felt left out if they rehearsed when I was around, but that day I was busy thinking about other things. The night before, I'd started writing a story about a group of friends in New York City who form a band and become famous. My brain was brimful of ideas about the characters, the drama, the plot twists. I'd tried to write books before and had always given up, but I was sure *this* was the one that would stick.

Then, right in the middle of a dance move, Caitlin spun around to look at me.

"You know, I was talking to Victoria in Maths and it turns out she's *never* kissed anyone. Can you believe that?"

Right away, my stomach began to sink. Sometimes

Caitlin would come out with odd thoughts out of nowhere or change conversations mid-sentence when she got bored of what we were talking about. But from the way she looked at Hannah, the tiny split-second smirks that flashed across their faces, I could tell that this wasn't random. They had planned to bring this up in front of me.

"It's not that weird," I said awkwardly. "Loads of people haven't kissed anybody yet."

"Seriously? She's almost fourteen." Caitlin's top lip curled. "It's a bit sad, don't you think?"

"Not really. I doubt Tilly or any of that group have kissed anyone, either."

I had no idea if that was true. Tilly Chan had been my best friend all through primary school, but she hung around with Jamie Singh and Elsie Jackson now. I always saw them together in the canteen or the corridors at break, usually playing some complicated board game or making their *Doctor Who* fanzine, but Tilly and I hadn't spoken in almost two years. She could have kissed a dozen people as far as I knew.

"Well, obviously. Who'd want to kiss any of those nerds?" Caitlin laughed. "No offence."

Hannah did a high kick and spun round. "Have *you* kissed anyone, Laurie?"

I hadn't. They knew I hadn't. I would have told them if I'd kissed someone – Hannah had her first kiss with a boy from her church youth group last year, and she went on about it for ages. She and Caitlin were trying to embarrass me. It wasn't the first time they'd done this: one time they made up a secret code for different bodily functions and spent a whole afternoon giggling at me when I unknowingly said I needed to fart.

I should have told them the truth. They might even have respected me for being honest, gone back to their dance routine and forgotten all about it. But I couldn't. I didn't care that I hadn't had my first kiss – until that moment, I'd hardly even thought about it. I just didn't want to give Caitlin the satisfaction of admitting it.

"Yeah, of course," I said, trying to keep my voice all light and casual. "I mean, only once. But yeah, I have."

"Oh yeah?" Hannah looked at Caitlin. "Who?"

"Just this boy I met when I was on holiday in Brighton last summer."

"What was his name?" Caitlin was grinning, and I realised with a kick of regret that I'd done exactly what she'd hoped I would. She wanted to trap me in a lie and make me squirm.

Instead of backing out, I said the first name that came into my head. It was the name of one of the characters in my new story – the one I most wished could hop off the page and actually be my friend.

"Neon Hart."

"Neon Hart?" Hannah laughed out loud. "His name was *Neon Hart*?"

"Yeah," I said, my voice squeaking a little. "He's American."

"So, you're telling us you kissed an American boy called *Neon Hart* on holiday and never even mentioned it?" Caitlin asked, adding quotation marks round his name with her fingers.

My throat was starting to get tight. I didn't understand Caitlin. Whenever I was alone with her, we had so much fun. She stayed over at my house twice while Hannah was in Italy for the Easter holidays, and it was everything a sleepover with your best friend was supposed to be. Caitlin told me about the boy she had a crush on, but she also talked about her parents' divorce last year, and we made my mums mad by banging around in the kitchen, baking marshmallow crispy squares at half past two in the morning.

But sometimes, when it was the three of us, she and Hannah ganged up on me like this. There was no way to know when it would happen or why. I just had to put up with it.

"I didn't know if you'd believe me." I threw my half-finished daisy chain into the grass. "You obviously don't, so I guess that was the right decision."

Caitlin's smile faded a little. My nonchalant act almost had her convinced. "OK, then. Let's see a photo."

"I don't have one," I said quickly. "I didn't take any, and his mum doesn't let him use social media."

"Oh, how convenient."

She laughed, any doubt she'd had that I was lying vanished. Hannah gave her a look, like it was time to wrap this up – she could never go as far with the teasing as Caitlin did.

Caitlin held up her hands in mock defeat. "OK, Laurie. If you say so."

I thought that would be the end of it. Instead, Neon became a running joke for Caitlin: she'd ask if I'd heard from him recently, or demand more details about our first kiss together. She never accused me outright of making the whole thing up, but it was clear she kept mentioning him because she wanted me to crack and admit it.

The harder she tried, the more determined I became not to. So I said I had his number and we spoke on the phone sometimes. I said the Statue of Liberty snow globe that Gio brought me back from a holiday to NYC three years ago was actually a gift from Neon. The longer my list of lies became, the harder they were to untangle. Soon it felt like there was no going back.

One day, I created an online profile for him. I posted photos of places around Manhattan and Brooklyn, things he had made or eaten, a pet dog that I named Cauliflower. And then, knowing that Caitlin and Hannah would go looking for them if I 'accidentally' left my phone unlocked, I began to send myself messages from his account. 'We' talked back and forth for ages, about everything: our families and friends, books and music and TV, the things that worried us or that we were scared of. It was partly like a diary, partly like a novel. I created a character with a life much more exciting than mine, in a big, shiny city that I'd only ever seen on a screen, but I poured all my own thoughts and feelings into it too.

I was even creating accounts for his made-up friends and relatives to make his profile look authentic. Caitlin still wasn't convinced he was real, but at some point it didn't matter. I'd stopped doing it for her. Neon had become someone I could rely on. He was always there to listen. I could tell him anything without worrying that he would laugh at me behind my back or use it against me later on. He may not have been real, but he felt like a real friend.

When I told Caitlin and Hannah that Neon was coming to visit me, it wasn't because they had been asking questions or teasing me about him – they hadn't even brought him up that day. I just wanted it to be true so badly, and I'd become so used to trying to prove to them that he was real that I let it slip out. I never actually planned to come to the station today. There are messages scheduled to arrive to my account from his in a few hours' time, saying that he's so, so sorry but his mum received some really bad news and they have to fly back to New York immediately.

But now … here he is, standing on the platform in front of me.

Caitlin and Hannah bombard Neon with questions, but I still haven't said anything. All I can do is stare at the birthmark above his eyebrow. If it wasn't for that, I might think that this was some horrible practical joke – that Caitlin had managed to track down a random boy who looked exactly like Neon, and could do a convincing New York accent, and had somehow persuaded him to come to Scotland to freak me out. But there's no faking that birthmark.

"Do you mind if we go and get something to eat?" Neon rubs his stomach. "I'm starving."

"Yeah, of course." Caitlin puts her hand on my arm. When she smiles at me now, it's genuine. "Do you want us to come too, Laurie?"

Somehow I manage to nod. I've wished that Neon was real lots of times. I've imagined what it would be like to actually have him in my life, a real person and not a figment of my imagination. In those daydreams, I always felt so happy to see him, but now I'm completely numb. Because, as I follow him and my friends out of the train station, the truth hits me: I have absolutely no idea who this boy is.

Four

Hannah's shooting-star earrings jingle as she shakes her head. "I can't believe you're actually here."

Ten minutes after Neon's arrival, we're sitting at a café in the shopping centre with half-drunk hot chocolates or frappuccinos in front of us (except Neon, who says he's all coffee'd out after the train and pulls a pack of shortbread from his backpack). I'm still too shocked to speak much – Hannah even had to order my drink for me – but my friends keep the conversation going with a million questions for Neon. They want to know what living in New York City is like, what he did while he was in London, how he got his mum to agree to him taking a solo trip to visit me while she stays in Edinburgh. Each of his answers matches exactly with the story I made up for him. Each of them makes me feel like I'm losing my mind.

Neon leans back in his seat. "I can't believe it, either. Laurie and I have talked about it for so long. It doesn't feel real."

He smiles at me. We're sitting beside each other, Caitlin and Hannah on the other side of the table, and I can't stop looking at him. I'm searching for a giveaway, something to prove that this boy isn't the Neon that I made up, because he can't be. But there's nothing. He's exactly like I pictured him, right down to the slightly chewed thumbnails.

Neon doesn't seem uncomfortable with my eagle-eyed stare, or surprised that I've barely uttered a word since he got here. I nod and open my mouth to say something now, but all that comes out is an unintelligible mumble.

"To tell you the truth," Caitlin says, "Hannah and I didn't think *you* were real."

Neon looks at her, his dark eyebrows rising slightly. "Oh, really? Why?"

"Well…" Caitlin waves her hand in a vague circle in front of him. "Your name, for one thing. And the fact you're from America."

Neon snorts. "OK, so my name *is* pretty uncommon. But what's unusual about being American? There are over three hundred million of us."

"Yeah, I know, but…" Caitlin is getting flustered. She looks at Hannah for backup, but Hannah is busy taking an extremely long sip of her hot chocolate. "It's hard to explain. It felt too good to be true, Laurie meeting someone like that."

Hearing her say that out loud makes me wince. Neon pokes himself in the chest, the cheek, the forehead, then looks back at Caitlin with a tight smile. "Nah. Definitely real. You should probably apologise to Laurie for calling her a liar, though."

He says this in such a cheerful tone that at first Caitlin and Hannah don't notice that he's criticising them. Their smiles falter.

"We never actually called her a liar," Caitlin says awkwardly.

"No, Neon's right." Hannah licks a smear of hot chocolate from her lower lip and looks at me. There actually is some regret in her large blue eyes. "I'm sorry, Laurie. We should have believed you."

Caitlin mumbles that she's sorry too. I don't know what to say. I *am* a liar, at least where this is concerned. I've told my friends hundreds of lies about Neon over the last six months. Though, when I was telling them, they didn't feel like lies. Neon had become almost as real to me as the kids in our class at school.

It's started to rain outside, so once we've finished our drinks we take a walk through the shopping centre. Neon seems weirdly fascinated by the place. He stops to stare at the decorative animal clock that moves and plays a tune every hour, looking far more amazed than any of the toddlers watching, then wanders into a homeware shop and spends twenty minutes admiring things like oven gloves and cake tins. If Caitlin and Hannah find it strange, they don't say so – he's cool enough to them to get away with being a bit quirky. Besides, they're never as critical with boys.

When we pass a make-up shop, I remind Hannah that she still needs to buy her mascara. She and Caitlin head inside while Neon and I linger by the entrance. As soon as my friends are out of earshot, I whirl round to face him. He's gazing at an advert for face cream like it's the *Mona Lisa*.

"What's going on?" I whisper. "What is this?"

Neon looks up from the poster. "What do you mean?"

"You know what I mean!" I hiss. I take a look around me, sure that someone else will be able to see something off about Neon. "I … I made you up. You're not real!"

When I created Neon's profile, I knew better than to steal some random person's pictures to pass off as his. It's way too easy to search for those online, and Caitlin would have found the original in five minutes. AI images weren't safe, either – there are websites that can detect those, and the program might give him six fingers or eight front teeth without my noticing.

Instead, I went on an app that filters photos to change people's appearance. I took some selfies and turned myself into a boy, making my face and lips thinner, my hair shorter and much darker, my eyes brown instead of blue. I added freckles and a birthmark shaped like France above my eyebrow. I smiled with my teeth, something I don't do much in photos, and wiped away the braces that I had back then. Neon Hart is me, painted with pixels.

"Um, OK, *ouch*." He laughs. "You did make me up, yes. But I'm here now. I think that makes me real enough."

That's not the response I expected. I don't know how I thought Neon would explain himself, but acknowledging that he did indeed come from my imagination was not it.

"But you can't be. You just can't."

Neon smiles and shrugs. Maybe I'm hallucinating, or stuck in a hyperrealistic dream. To test my theory, I try to slice my hand through his body, the way people do with ghosts in films. My fingers bump against his arm. It's not hard but Neon put his hand on his bicep and winces dramatically.

"Again: ouch!"

"But h-how?" I say, stumbling over the words. "What do you mean, real enough?"

"I'll explain everything later, I promise. There are too many people around right now, and I don't want your friends to overhear." He puts his hands on my shoulders and gives them a soft shake. "Come on, Laurie, lighten up. Aren't you even a bit happy to see me?"

Despite the smile, he sounds hurt. I'm too busy working through *stunned* and *confused* and *worried I'm having a breakdown* to get anywhere close to *happy* right now, but it would be rude to tell Neon that.

"Of course I am. It's just … where are you going to stay?"

Neon frowns. "What do you mean? I thought I was staying at yours?"

"My family don't know about you!"

"But you said your moms would be away all week." He beams. "So it's perfect timing."

"They haven't left yet. Besides, my brother's going to be at home the whole time." The thought of trying to explain any of this to Joel makes my cheeks burn. He'd think I'd completely lost it. "Look, I'm really sorry, but can't you … go back? Your mum's still in Edinburgh, right? You could get the train back down and…"

Neon's face clouds over. "Are you serious? I came here for you, saved you from looking like a compulsive liar in front of your friends, and you're telling me to get lost five minutes later? You're supposed to be *my* friend too, you know."

I feel a rush of guilt. If this boy really is Neon, then he must actually believe we're friends. All the long conversations we had, the thousands of messages swapping stories and songs and secrets – somehow, to him, they were real. If I'd come this far to see a friend and they were acting the way I am now, I'd be really upset too.

"I'm sorry. I *am* happy you're here. I just … wasn't expecting for it to actually happen." I glance into the shop and see Caitlin and Hannah walking back towards us, both holding paper carrier bags. "Of course you can come back to mine. We'll work something out."

Neon nods, his eyes still fixed on the poster in front of him. For a moment, I worry that Caitlin and Hannah will pick up on the tension between Neon and me, but then he asks what they bought and laughs when Caitlin shows him some ridiculously huge false eyelashes, and the atmosphere clears so quickly it's like our disagreement never happened.

Five

At four o'clock, I remember my promise to Mutti that I would be home before she and Mum go to the airport. Hannah still has some stuff to buy, so Neon and I leave her and Caitlin at the shopping centre and hurry off to the bus station. We almost miss the number seventeen because Neon keeps stopping to look at things: the front window of a health-food shop, a statue of a unicorn, a tiny chihuahua yapping outside a newsagent's...

"This place must seem really boring compared to New York," I say.

I've never left Europe, but I spent so long looking up photos and information about Neon's neighbourhood that I feel like I've been there. I picked it because I liked the name – Alphabet City. I read reviews of local businesses to choose Neon's favourite deli and ice-cream shop. I looked up timetables to find which bus or subway lines he would take to get to different places, found photos from parks and beautiful brownstone buildings to post to his account, then edited them slightly so they couldn't be easily reverse-searched. I could write a guidebook about somewhere that I've never even been.

"You only think this place is boring because you're so used to it." Neon leans down to inspect some dandelions growing round the foot of a lamp post. "It doesn't look like that to me. It's really different than – hey, check that out!"

He spots a snail among the weeds and tries to pick it up, but I hurry him towards the station and join the queue of people waiting to get the bus back to our town. Before we reach the front of the line, Neon clears his throat.

"So, minor problem. I don't have any money."

"You don't?" That explains why he didn't buy anything at the café, even after saying he was hungry. "How did you get on the train without any money?"

"It's, um, hard to explain… Do you have enough for the both of us?"

I count out the change in my pocket and fortunately have enough for another half single. We go upstairs, which is quiet apart from a few older kids sprawled out on the back seats. Neon wants to sit right at the front, and he actually does a little excited bounce as the bus pulls away from the kerb. You'd think he'd never been on public transport before.

"So?" I say, once we're moving. "Are you going to tell me now?"

"Look! That dog and its owner are wearing matching shoes!" He taps at the window so hard that the woman looks up, startled. Neon laughs and turns to face me. "Sorry, what were you saying?"

I glance round to make sure the kids at the back aren't listening. They're all watching something on a phone and aren't paying us any attention. "You said you'd explain."

"Explain what?"

"How you're here!" I say, exasperated.

Even in our made-up conversations, Neon could be quite frustrating – he was forever getting distracted and changing the subject. But at least I could always tell him when he was being annoying, unlike my other friends.

"Do I have to?" He flings his arms out in a *ta-da!* motion. "I'm here now. Does it really matter how it happened?"

"Yes, it matters!" The words come out a little too loud. When I glance over my shoulder again, a few of the kids at the back are looking at us. "I feel like I'm losing my mind. This is impossible. I *made you up*."

Neon sits back and crosses his arms, pouting slightly. His attitude is a bit like Joel's whenever Mum or Mutti tries to explain something like a new bookkeeping system for the shop – that this is a very boring task that he has to suffer through before getting back to more interesting things.

"OK. So, yes, technically you made me up. Thank you for that, by the way." Neon gives an exaggerated bow to show his gratitude. I frown, trying to get him to be serious, and at last he drops the joking tone. "When you created me, if that's what you want to call it, I arrived in a place called... Well, there are lots of names for it, in all different languages. Some people call it the Land of Make-believe, but most of us think that sounds too childish. Others are trying to make Fictionalia stick, but I'm not a fan of that. Let's call it the Realm."

It takes me a few seconds to digest his words. "The Realm. OK." When he doesn't continue, I ask, "And what is this realm?"

"It's the place where fictional creations live. All of us.

Every single person or character that's ever been made up is there."

"All of them? Every single one?" I root around in my foggy brain for a story. The first that comes to mind is a film I was obsessed with at age six. "So, like … Elsa from *Frozen*? She lives there too?"

"I'm sure she does, though I don't know her personally," Neon says with a laugh. "There are millions of us. Billions, probably."

"Right." My mouth has gone dry. I swallow and try to make sense of what he's saying. There's no way it can be true, but I decide to go along with it for now. "So, how are you here, then?"

"Sometimes, not often, we can cross over into your world."

Neon looks through the window: at the blurry halos of drizzle round car headlights, the umbrellas gliding above pavements.

"Not everyone can do it. It's only possible when someone in this world really, really believes in us. It usually happens to characters from little kids' books or shows. There was a major issue with the Gruffalo turning up at a birthday party in Manchester last year, apparently."

I stare at him, waiting for him to crack and admit this is all one big joke. It doesn't happen. Neon is smiling but his tone is calm and straightforward, as if he's describing a town down the road and not the ridiculous story he's presented me with.

"But I knew you were fake," I whisper. "I invented you."

"You did. But you started to believe in me, right?" His dark eyes glimmer. "It was only for a few seconds, but it was there. I could feel it. You started to believe I was real."

He's right. There were moments when I'd get a notification for a new post from Neon's account and forget that I was the one running it. Sometimes I'd see something funny or interesting and think, *I should send this to Neon*, as if there was anyone other than me behind the account. It's sad to admit it but I'd often scroll through our old 'conversations' and laugh at the things 'we' had said.

The truth is I wanted someone like Neon. I wanted a friendship group like the one I gave him with his band – people that I could trust completely instead of worrying whether today was going to be one of the Bad Days when they ganged up on me and made fun of me. I wanted someone who I could tell my secrets to without worrying that they'd spill them or use them against me. Someone who got me, who made me feel like the funniest and smartest and best version of myself. Even if we argued sometimes, even if we didn't always agree.

I used to have that. But Tilly doesn't talk to me any more.

"Plus, I'd bet a lot of the people you added to my social accounts believe that I'm real – you did a really good job making those profiles seem authentic. So that, plus your belief and…" He does jazz hands. "Voila! I'm here."

"I see."

But I don't. I don't get how any of this is possible. Out of ideas, I slump in my seat and let his words whirl round my mind. There must be a logical explanation somewhere, but I can't find it. My head is starting to hurt from trying.

The bus slips through the outskirts of the city and towards the villages dotted along the loch. Neon gets excited by cows, a billboard for a distillery and the steam billowing from a factory. I can't help but smile when he shrieks at the sight of a seagull – his joy is pretty infectious. But the closer we come to our town, the more nervous I feel.

"So, um, how long are you staying again?"

"Calm down, dude. I'm not planning on moving in." Neon rolls his eyes. "Only a week. Any longer and people will notice that I've gone. I'll leave next Saturday, before your moms get back from their trip."

"What people? People in the Realm?" I ask. Neon nods, and there's a little hint of worry in his expression. "Will you get in trouble? Aren't you supposed to leave?"

"Um, no. There'll be hell to pay if anyone realises I'm gone. I'm only staying a little while, though, so it shouldn't be an issue. I'll be back before they even notice."

He gestures grandly to the window, like he's pointing out the Niagara Falls or Mount Everest and not some soggy field on the outskirts of Inverness.

"Besides, I've never been to the real world before, and this is probably my only chance. I want to make the most of every moment."

Six

It's getting dark by the time we arrive back at my town. We get off the bus on the high street and walk past the bookshop where Gio is finishing up for the night. There are a dozen or so customers milling around the tables, which is a relief – on Wednesday no one came in all day.

Neon points to the Halloween display in the window. "This is your moms' bookstore, right? Can we go in?"

I almost ask him how he knows that, then remember I've told him all about my life in our messages. Neon probably knows me better than anyone else in the world.

"Not right now. I need to be home before five, and I'll have to work out what to tell Gio about you first."

My family lives a few minutes away from the shop, in a semi-detached house with a blue door and a very overgrown back garden. I pause on the corner of our street, working out how to sneak Neon past my mums. We don't have a garage or a shed that he can hide in, and it wouldn't be fair to ask him to crouch in the downstairs cupboard until they leave.

"Here's what we're going to do," I whisper. "We'll … we'll run upstairs to my room really fast and hope they don't follow."

He bursts out laughing. "That's your brilliant idea? Stellar work, Laurie. I've seen multiple James Bonds in action in the Realm, and none of them have anything on you."

"Well, I don't know what else to do," I say, throwing my arms up. "Do you want to wait here until they leave?"

"Uh, I'd rather not. It's pretty cold out here." He wraps his arms round himself and shivers. "Next time, imagine me as the owner of a very thick winter coat, OK?"

I creep forward to make sure that our next-door neighbour, Carrie, isn't peeking through her front windows, then open the gate and beckon for Neon to follow me down the path to our house. I push the front door open, quietly slip off my shoes, then pull him upstairs and into my bedroom as quickly as I can. Neon spins round to take it in.

"I can't believe I'm actually here," he says, his eyes twinkling. "It's smaller than I imagined, but it's cosy."

My room is nothing special – four sky-blue walls, a bed and a desk, a beige carpet that's constantly covered with books and clothes – but the way he looks around, you'd think this was the big reveal on one of the interior-design shows that my mum likes so much. I hold my finger to my lips, then creep back to the door. No footsteps follow us. We're safe.

I pull the curtains closed and gesture to the bed. "Stay here and don't make any noise."

Neon sits down and salutes. "Aye aye, cap'n."

Heart pounding, I leave him looking around and slip out on to the landing. My heart almost leaps out of my chest when I see Mum just in front of me, dressed in her big coat and scarf and struggling down the stairs with a suitcase. She pushes her hair out of her face and looks up at me with a smile.

"Oh, good, you're home. The taxi will be here in five minutes."

Hurrying away from my bedroom, I grab the handle of the suitcase and help her downstairs. Mutti is standing at the front door, adjusting her bright red bobble hat. The tension between her and Mum seems to have disappeared for now. Whatever the issue is, maybe a week in London will help.

"Have a good time," I tell them, trying to steady the tremor in my voice. "Good luck for your events, Mutti."

Mum starts going over the rules for the week, including that I have to leave my phone downstairs before I go to bed. Right then, I remember the posts that I've got scheduled to go up on Neon's main account. I whip out my phone and open the app to delete them – Caitlin and Hannah both follow Neon, and they'd be really confused if they saw those.

"There's money in the elephant teapot for a takeaway. *One* takeaway. Try to eat at least semi-healthily the rest of the time, please. Five a day, and all that." Mum waves a hand in front of my phone. "Are you listening, Laurie?"

I nod but don't look up – I'm sure she'll notice something is wrong if she looks me in the eye. "Five takeaways a day. Got it."

Mum chuckles and swats at me with the end of her scarf. "Remember to lock the back door if you're both going out. Call Gio if there are any issues at the shop. Oh, and absolutely no parties."

She shouts that last part through to the kitchen, where Joel is sitting at the table. He gestures to his laptop and the pile of textbooks beside him. "Do I look like I have time for parties? I've got three assignments due next week, and I haven't done the reading for two of them."

"They'll be fine, Liv." Mutti picks up her coat from the end of the bannister and eases her arms into it. "And Carrie's around if there are any emergencies."

Joel joins us in the hallway. "Carrie will *definitely* know if there are any emergencies."

A loud voice calls from outside. "I heard that!"

Our next-door neighbour Carrie is without a doubt one of the world's nosiest people. It would be more annoying if she wasn't so nice – she's always coming over to our house with food or newspaper clippings about Mutti's books, and she's got a random and ridiculous story for every occasion. She's sitting on her front step when we follow Mum and Mutti out to the car, a cup of tea in her hand and a book that is probably a cover for her eavesdropping in her lap.

"Is that you off to London, then, Monika?" she asks Mutti. "Sounds so fancy. You're like literary royalty."

Mutti wheels her suitcase down the garden path and laughs. "We're staying in a two-star hotel and will probably eat Tesco meal deals all week, so not quite."

"Still – London!" Carrie says dreamily. "Did I ever tell you I lived in a houseboat on the Thames one summer? With a painter from Tuscany and a goat named Sally."

She launches into one of her stories, but this time I'm too nervous to listen. Upstairs, the curtains of my bedroom window twitch. My heart leaps, but luckily Mum and Mutti are too busy laughing at Carrie's account of the time the Tuscan painter and the goat got stuck in the toilet together to notice anything. A moment later, the taxi pulls up by the pavement.

"Right! Be good, duckies." Mutti still calls us that, even though I'm fourteen and Joel is nineteen. She gives me a tight hug before scurrying over to him. Mum does the same, then they load their suitcases into the boot and climb into the taxi. We all wave goodbye, Carrie raising her cup of tea into the air like she's making a toast.

"Pop round whenever if you need anything, you two," she tells us as the car slips out of view. "I've got Pilates on Monday and Wednesday evenings, and my friend has asked me to keep an eye on their bonsai collection while they're shooting a film in Thailand. But apart from that I'll be around all week."

Carrie works from home, so she's almost always in. That could make getting Neon in and out of the house without being spotted tricky, but I'll worry about that when the time comes. I thank her, then race back upstairs to my room. Neon is crouching by my chest of drawers and rifling through my old notebooks and pens.

"Er, what are you doing?" I hurry over and shut the drawer – I've got some diaries from when I was eight or nine in there that I would rather die than let anyone see, even made-up people like Neon.

"Sorry, I got too curious." He holds up a purple pencil case that I haven't seen in forever. "Stuff is so much more *real* here. The colours are brighter and it feels different, and—"

"You have to be quiet! Joel is downstairs."

I open my computer and turn on some music so that Joel

can't hear us talking, but that makes Neon bounce to his feet, shouting that he's obsessed with this song. According to the story I made up about him, he loves singing, like me, and he also plays guitar and piano and a bunch of other instruments. I turn the music up and put a finger to my lips. Neon begins to lip-synch along to the song instead, but the floorboards creak with his enthusiastic dance moves.

"What are we going to do?" I run my hands over my face and sigh. "You can't stay here until Saturday."

"I think I sort of have to?" He smiles apologetically. "Reminder: you *did* invite me."

"Yeah, but I didn't think you'd actually – never mind." I shake my head. "How about a hotel? There are a few B&Bs in town – you could try one of those."

"No money, remember?" Neon pats the purple backpack lying on my bed. "Look. Empty. You should have imagined me as a millionaire."

He laughs but that gives me an idea.

"Could I start now? Not necessarily a millionaire – but what if I imagined you had loads more money?"

"It doesn't work now that I'm out of the Realm," Neon says. "Back there, you could have made me the richest person in the world, or a dragon or a koala bear or whatever you fancied. Remember when you changed my birthday? That was quite confusing."

Originally I'd decided on the middle of June for Neon's birthday, but then I realised that would make him a Gemini. I'm Pisces, so I shifted it back a few weeks to make him a Cancer so we'd be more compatible as friends. It seems silly now – I don't even really believe in star signs, but I figured that Neon would.

"What about your mum?" She flashes into my head as soon as I mention her – a tall, willowy hippy who I named Karma. "Can we get her to come here? She'd have some money, surely."

Neon sits up and takes a turquoise pen from the pot on my desk. "Not possible. You never believed in my mom the way you started to believe in me, and she didn't have loads of online followers who thought she was real. Besides, we don't have any way to contact her there."

I sink on to the bed beside him, out of ideas and out of energy. There's a big part of me that wants to call my mums and get them to turn the taxi round, come home and sort this out for me, but I can't. These events are a big deal for Mutti, and there's no way they'd believe any of this anyway. Neon flops back, already at home in my space – the very space where I spent so long imagining him, talking to him, wishing he was real.

"Chill out, Laur. It's only a week." He twirls the pen in his fingers and grins. "How much could go wrong?"

Seven

With Neon here, my room feels more cramped than usual. Physically he's not much bigger than me, but something about him takes up a lot of space. Maybe it's the fact that he moves so much. He gets up and down from my bed a dozen times; he dances to the songs he likes and leaps across the room when he wants to look at something – and he wants to look at *everything*. He goes through my books, the shoes shoved in the bottom of my cupboard, then stares at the photos of my family and friends pinned on the corkboard above my desk.

"You didn't tell me you had a pet!" he says, pointing to a photo of nine-year-old me cuddling a beautiful cocker spaniel.

"We don't," I say sadly. "That's Bella. She's my friend Tilly's dog. Well, my ex-friend."

"Oh. Sorry." He flops on to the bed beside me. I shuffle over to make room. "I wish I could have brought Cauliflower. She would have loved to meet you."

I shift against my pillows. "Cauliflower actually lives in the Realm with you?"

He looks at me like I've asked if the Earth is round.

"Of course she does. Where else would she live?"

"Does that mean all the characters I made up are there?" The amount of people I created to make sure Neon looked real was ridiculous. "What about the rest of the band? Kairo and Jennie and Yifei – are they all there too?"

"Yeah, of course they are. Like I said, anyone fictional. Even characters that people make up in their heads — lots of imaginary friends and monsters from under beds. They're pretty cute, actually."

I stare at Neon for a long moment. Part of me still expects him to burst out laughing and admit this is a huge joke, but it doesn't happen. Instead, I feel myself starting to believe him. None of it makes sense … and yet it's the only logical explanation as to how he could be in my room right now.

There are a million questions I want to ask but, before I can work out where to start, footsteps creak on the stairs. Joel has an annoying habit of barging into my room without knocking, so I rush out on to the landing before he has the chance and slam the door behind me. He pauses on the top step, one hand on the bannister.

"What are you hiding in there?"

"Nothing!" My voice comes out in a squeak. I'm not doing a good job of acting casual. "Did you want something?"

Joel and I are technically half-siblings. Mutti gave birth to him, then Mum had me five years later. They used the same donor, so we are biologically related, but you can't tell by looking at us. Mum has blond hair and blue eyes, like me, and Mutti is a very pale brunette, but Joel has dark brown hair and his eyes are almost black. They linger on my door now, full of curiosity.

But then his expression clears. "I was going to order a takeaway. What do you feel like?"

I tell him to get whatever he wants, which is also suspicious – last year, our parents left us alone for three days while they went to a book festival, and we had a full-blown argument because we couldn't decide between Indian and Chinese food.

After a moment, Joel shrugs. "Thai it is, then. Green curry, yeah?"

I mumble that curry sounds good and rush back into my bedroom. Barely half an hour of hiding Neon and my anxiety is already through the roof – I don't know how I'm going to keep this up until Saturday.

Neon looks up at me as I come in. "Can I have some of your curry? I'm starving."

"Yeah, yeah," I whisper, sitting down on the bed. "But listen, we need to think of a plan. How about…"

"Ha!"

The door slams open and Joel jumps into my room. There's an annoying, triumphant grin on his face, but it vanishes when he sees the boy sitting beside me. "Laurie, who…"

"This is really not what it looks like," I say, which is true. Whatever Joel is thinking, it could not possibly be anything close to the reality of the situation.

"What's going on here?" Joel asks, looking from me to Neon and back. "Who are you?"

"You must be Joel." Neon stands up and offers his hand for Joel to shake. It's so formal that I'd laugh if I wasn't terrified about what he might say next. "I'm Neon. I'm a friend of Laurie's. I'm visiting from New York City."

"Neon?" Joel repeats. "Visiting as in staying here? In our house?"

"Yes," Neon says, right as I say, "No!"

Joel asks which it is, so I reluctantly change my answer to a yes. He's here now. It's not like I can kick him out. Deep down, I don't want to, either.

"It's only for a few days," I say. "Until Friday."

"Let me get this straight. You invited your friend from *New York* to visit without checking with Mum and Mutti?" Joel asks. When I nod, he bursts out laughing. "Laurie, this is ridiculous. How did you two even meet?"

"In Brighton last summer. Mum and Mutti let me go to the arcades on the pier by myself for a bit, and we got talking there."

Joel didn't come with us on that trip, so I can stick to the story I told Caitlin and Hannah. My parents would know it's a lie – they and their friends were always around when we went to the pier, so there was no time for me to go making friends with other tourists – but Neon will be gone before they come home.

"Well, as long as you're not inviting random people off the internet into our house. What about your parents? Are they OK with you coming all this way by yourself?" Joel asks Neon.

Neon nods quickly. "Yeah, my mom likes to give me a lot of freedom. She's a bit alternative. I mean, she named me *Neon*," he adds with a laugh. It's the exact same joke I wrote into my story about him months ago, and it makes my head spin to hear him repeat it now.

"All right, then." Joel crosses his arms and raises his eyebrows at me. "You know, I'm quite impressed. I didn't think you'd be into the whole teenage rebellion thing, but sneaking a long-distance boyfriend into the house while Mum and Mutti are away…"

My face heats up. "He's not my boyfriend!"

"Uh-huh. Sure." Joel grins. "Well, even so, he obviously can't sleep in your room. You can set up the sofa bed downstairs for him."

"I'll do it." Neon jumps to his feet. "Thanks a lot for letting me stay."

"It's not like I have much of a choice, do I? I can hardly kick you out on to the street." Joel turns to leave, then pauses. "I'm guessing you'll need feeding too. Are you all right with Thai food?"

He passes over his phone for Neon to select from the menu on the restaurant app. I watch his fingers paw at the screen and feel slightly dizzy at the sight: Neon, real and solid and *here*, discussing the difference between tom yum goong and tom kha gai with my brother.

"Are you going to tell Mum?" I ask Joel.

Mutti I'm not so worried about – she'd probably think this was hilarious. Mum is a different story. She would ground me for the next 3,000 years. And she'd definitely want to phone Neon's mother, and what would we do then?

I expect Joel to make me pay for his silence, like the time I left the lid off the blender and soaked Mum's brand-new coffee machine with strawberry smoothie. I had to promise to cook him pancakes every day for a week before he'd help me tidy up. At the very least, he's going to dangle the threat of telling our parents about Neon over me until next Saturday.

But instead Joel shakes his head. "Nah. They've got a lot on. I don't want them worrying about this too." He raises his eyebrows before turning to the door. "Just try to stay out of trouble – and no more surprise visitors."

Eight

Neon wants to see more of our town, so after breakfast on Sunday I give him a tour. To be honest, there's not all that much to look at, especially now that half the high street has closed down. It always feels quite depressing to walk past the spots where I used to spend ages picking out sweets or debating which toy to spend my pocket money on, and see only vacant plots in their place. The town feels quieter than it did when I was little. Sadder somehow.

Neon, though, seems delighted by everything we pass, from the faded red letter box outside the post office to the sign about a missing cat in the chip-shop window. We pass Every Book & Cranny again, but we can't go in since Gio doesn't open until eleven on Sundays. Instead, we stop by the pet shop, Bohemian Catsody. Tilly used to joke that the owner, Martha, and my parents were competing to find the high street's worst pun. Neon is so amazed by the tanks of tropical fish that it makes Martha laugh out loud.

"Do they not have fish where you come from?"

She's a small woman, probably around thirty, with blue-rimmed glasses and pastel-pink hair. My mums love her – she's a romcom addict and one of our best customers at

Every Book & Cranny.

"Yeah, but not like this." Neon's eyes dart about as he follows a tiny flash of electric blue round the tank. "They're so *bright*."

"I'd give you one to take home, but I don't think it'd like the plane much." Martha points to a small silvery fish with streaks of vivid blue and orange along its body. "This one would be perfect for you. It's called a neon tetra."

"No way!" Neon grabs my arm. "Let's get some! Look, you can get ten for eight pounds! Is that a lot?"

I don't have a fish bowl, enough money to buy one or the nerve to discover how Joel would react if I came home with ten new pets, so I say goodbye to Martha and drag Neon from the shop. Next, we take a walk round the park – the play area is full of little kids, which is lucky as I have a feeling Neon would want to spend hours on the swings otherwise – and then head to my favourite bakery. When Robbie, the owner, hears Neon speak, his eyes light up.

"Wow, your accent – that's more New York than a yellow taxi." He sets down a tray of white rolls and brushes the flour from his tattooed hands. "I've got cousins over there, been to visit them five or six times. Which area are you from?"

My shoulders tense as Neon and Robbie start chatting about Manhattan and Brooklyn and Queens. If Neon is exactly like I created him, then everything he knows about New York City must be based on my research. I'm nervous that he'll say something completely wrong, and Robbie will realise Neon is no more of a New Yorker than I am. Luckily they mostly talk about baseball games and pastrami sandwiches, then Robbie throws in a couple of misshapen doughnuts with our order of two Chelsea buns. Neon digs into a doughnut the moment we're out of the shop.

"Man, food is so much tastier here in the real world." He takes a second bite, leaving a ring of powdered sugar round his mouth. "Weird that you have to pay for it, though. We take whatever we want in the Realm. It reappears a few moments later anyway."

"So, how does it work exactly?" I ask, lowering my voice even though the street is nearly empty. "Since I decided you live in New York, is that what the Realm looks like for you?"

Neon shakes his head. "No, the life you gave me is more like a memory. Once we've been created, we enter the Realm with the personality and backstory that the person has made up for us. That way we can interact with characters from all sorts of worlds, even ones totally different to this. One of my best friends there is a centaur," he says as casually as if he'd said they were Dutch or a Sagittarius.

"But what does the Realm actually look like, then?" I try to imagine a place where dragons and talking animals mingle with ordinary characters from literary novels like Mutti's. It sounds totally chaotic.

"It changes all the time. Sometimes it's like any other city, sometimes a dramatic fantasy landscape, sometimes futuristic. There are always really amazing sunsets – the romance characters love those." Neon nudges a crumpled Coke can on the pavement with his toe. "And I gotta say it's a lot cleaner than the real world."

We keep wandering and a few minutes later arrive at the edge of Loch Ness. Its legendary monster has probably made it one of the most famous lakes in the country, maybe in Europe, but our part of it isn't so remarkable: a long, wide stretch of water with pine trees on the other side. Even so, I really like coming here. Tilly and I used to walk Bella along the water's edge all the time. We carved our names under one of the benches when we were ten: *Tilly & Laurie forever!* tucked inside an oddly shaped flower. It feels strange when Neon stops at the exact same spot.

"So this is home to the Loch Ness Monster." Neon grabs a Chelsea bun from the paper bag and takes a large bite. "Ever spotted her?"

"Not yet." I sit down on the bench, then spin round to look at him. "Wait, have *you*? She must live in the Realm too, right?"

"I guess she must, but I've never seen her. Sounds like she's the secretive type." He raises his eyebrows. "A bit like you."

"Me? I don't think I'm secretive." I push my hair behind my ears and shake my head. "Except for this whole story with you, but that's different."

Only that's not entirely true. There are plenty of things that I haven't told Caitlin and Hannah about myself, even after being friends with them for two years. Sometimes it's because I worry they'd make fun of me, like the fact I love the über-cheesy German pop music that Mutti plays in the car, but sometimes I don't think they'd be interested, like in the novels I've tried to write. I used to tell my parents almost everything, but lately I've been keeping lots of things from them too. They don't know quite how mean my friends can be. They don't know how sad I've felt a lot of the past two years.

Even in my made-up conversations with Neon, I wasn't

totally open about my life. I didn't tell him anything about Tilly, for one thing. When I was talking to him, I could pretend that I was someone different, someone funny and bright and popular. Not the girl whose best friend dumped her as soon as they started secondary school. Not the girl whose new friends barely seem to like her some days.

"You didn't even tell me you could sing," Neon says.

My cheeks instantly heat up. "How do you know I like singing?"

"I heard you belting out Taylor Swift in the shower this morning. You're really good!"

Part of me wants to die of embarrassment, but another part is happy to get the compliment. Caitlin and Hannah have no idea that I can sing. Hardly anyone has ever heard me before. Mum and Mutti always say I'm good, but they're biased.

"Maybe you're right," I tell Neon, my eyes fixed on the shiny dark surface of the loch. "Maybe I'm more secretive than I realised."

Neon takes another bite of bun, then lightly slaps my knee.

"That must be my purpose!" he shouts through a mouthful of half-chewed pastry. "I'm a fictional character, right? So, if I've turned up in your life like this, it's obviously for a reason. Maybe I'm supposed to bring you out of your shell. Make you see that it's OK to be you, just the way you are, or something heart-warming like that."

"I'm not sure that's how it works now you're in the real world," I say, laughing. "But sure, you can try. Maybe I'll be a totally different person by Saturday."

He shakes his head. "I don't want you to be totally different. More like ... Laurie Plus. Laurie the Deluxe Edition! Featuring brand-new confidence and extra sparkle."

I roll my eyes and bump my shoulder against his, but a smile tugs at my lips. Laurie the Deluxe Edition doesn't sound bad at all.

Nine

I'd thought I'd leave Neon at home when I went to school the next day, but Joel vetoes that plan before I've even finished breakfast.

"No way. I'm working in the shop all day, and then I've got to get back to my essays. I don't have time to babysit."

"Neon's fourteen!" I protest through a mouthful of toast. "He doesn't need babysitting."

"It's OK. Honestly I'd much rather go to school."

Neon shovels another spoonful of Crunchy Nut into his mouth. For someone who's not technically real, he eats a *lot*. Last night he got through three servings of the veggie lasagne that Mutti left in the freezer, and then scarfed down two chocolate bars as dessert.

"I've been home-schooled my whole life. I'd love to see what a high school is like."

"But…" I trail off, kicking myself for deciding to make him home-schooled back when I created him. The thought of bringing Neon to school makes me feel slightly sick. It's like revealing a part of my own soul, letting this person that I made up walk around with the kids in my class.

"OK." I sigh. "We need to find you something to wear."

Fortunately Joel inherited Mum's inability to ever throw anything away, so he rescues his old school jumper and trousers from the back of his cupboard and lends them to Neon.

Neon goes to the bathroom to change and comes out with a big grin on his face. "What do you think? Will I fit in?"

I nod, though I already know that he won't. There's something magnetic about Neon, something that attracts attention. This is a small town and there aren't that many pupils at our school, so anyone new tends to stick out. Some people in my year follow Neon's profiles, so they'll know who he is – Caitlin and Hannah must have told them about him. I wonder who else in our class thinks I'm a compulsive liar. Despite the anxiety, the prospect of being able to prove them wrong makes me smile.

There's a spring in Neon's step as we make our way up our street and towards school. He half walks, half dances down the road, bouncing on his heels and singing to himself, apart from a few seconds when he stops to examine a ladybird.

"I'm excited!" he says for the eighth or ninth time since we left the house. "I've always wanted to experience a normal school. I talked to my mom about going when I was ten or eleven, but she thinks the state system doesn't leave enough room for creativity, you know? Well, of course you know. You made it up."

He laughs. I wonder if this is weird for him, meeting the person who decided everything about his persona. After I created his online profiles, I tried to keep Neon's story straightforward so it seemed more believable. Sometimes, though, it was hard not to give in to the pull of drama and excitement – his dad is a pilot who walked out on his family when Neon was two, and his mum taught Neon herself while they travelled around Asia and South America before settling back in New York City a few years ago.

My life has always been so normal. I've only ever lived in this town, and the only times I've been abroad were a couple of visits to see my uncle and cousins in Hamburg. It was fun to make up a story about someone who'd seen so much of the world.

"You won't tell anyone where you've come from, will you?" I ask. "Especially not Caitlin or Hannah."

"Of course I won't. It's not a good idea to let too many humans know about the Realm." He swings his arms. "Otherwise people could force themselves to believe in all sorts of creatures and bring them here."

"They could? That sounds messy."

Neon is one thing – he looks like any other teenager – but monsters or mythological creatures would have a much harder time blending in.

"Tell me about it," Neon says. "Fanfic has made things complicated too. People make up stories about celebrities, but it's not who they really are, only their idea of them. Last year, there was a girl in Wales who actually managed to manifest a fictionalised version of her favourite singer. Luckily it was passed off as a very good lookalike, but it was a close call – a lot of people were asking why Jung Kook was looking at kitchen tongs in a supermarket in Llandudno."

I blink at him. "OK. Well, let's try to avoid any other … unexpected visitors."

"Unexpected visitors? You keep forgetting that *you* invited *me* here. In my world, that was real. I didn't think it would be such an inconvenience for you." He laughs but the hurt in his voice makes guilt nip at my skin.

"It's not that I'm not happy you're here," I say quickly. "Of course I am. But it's not as simple as that."

"It could be." He puts his arm round my shoulders and shakes them lightly. "No one is going to find out that you made me up, I promise. Who would even believe it if they did?"

~

A few people stare at Neon as we walk through the gates. I'd feel intimidated by that, especially never having been to school before, but Neon seems unfazed: he kicks a stray ball back towards a group of first years when it rolls our way, and shouts a loud hello to three girls in the year above me who are looking at him and whispering. I lead him to reception and ask Mr Jamieson if it's OK if Neon joins me in class today.

"I have a letter from his mum to say it's fine," I add quickly. I knew we'd be asked for that, so before we left this morning Neon and I wrote a letter on Joel's laptop, printed it out and signed it Karma Hart. Mr Jamieson grumbles a bit – apparently I should have asked weeks ago – but he eventually asks Neon to sign the guest entrance register and hands over a visitor's badge. Neon clips it on to his school jumper proudly.

"Can you take a photo of me?" he asks.

He pulls a bunch of cheesy poses outside reception while I take photos on my phone. The kids around us are making no effort to hide their stares. When he smiles back at a group of first-year girls, they all burst into giggles and hurry away like flustered ducklings.

The corridor is filling up now. I lead Neon towards the spot where I always meet Caitlin and Hannah before registration. It feels a bit like shepherding a toddler – Neon wanders into the Art classroom to take a look at a row of self-portraits pinned to the wall, and I have to steer him away from the canteen when he smells the bacon sandwiches left over from breakfast.

Caitlin and Hannah are in the upstairs corridor talking to Hari and Russell, who are in 3C with us. The boys both do a double take when they see Neon.

"You're Laurie's American friend!" Hari points at Neon. "We all thought she made you up!"

"See!" Caitlin shouts, beaming. "I told you he was real."

"I thought he was a catfish." Russell gawps at Neon for a long moment. "You don't *look* like you're fifty."

My cheeks go bright red. "Of course he's not fifty. Don't be gross, Russell."

"Definitely fourteen. Definitely real." Neon waves as Hannah introduces them both. "Hi. I'm visiting for the week."

"He's from New York City," Caitlin tells the boys. She sounds quite proud to have a friend from there, which bugs me – forty-eight hours ago, she didn't even think he was real, and now she's acting like they're old pals. "Is this your first time in a real school, Neon? You're home-schooled, right?"

Neon tells them about how he's always been taught by his mum, making them laugh with stories of some of her more eccentric lessons – for a while, she had him doing an online course in an artificial language called Esperanto, which she was sure was going to make a big comeback. (That's actually something Carrie said once. I think she might have been trying to wind Mutti up, though.)

Across the corridor, Tilly is sitting on a bench with her group. Jamie and Elsie have their books open and are doing some last-minute homework, but Tilly is staring right at Neon. Her mouth is open and her face has gone pale, a perfect reflection of the shock that I felt on Saturday. She looks at me, and a jolt of fear moves through me. It's as if Tilly knows this shouldn't be possible. Like she knows that I lied.

I take a breath to steady my nerves. There's no way Tilly could have guessed the truth. Most likely she thought I was getting catfished, same as Russell and Hari. I give her a small, smug smile before turning away. I shouldn't care what Tilly thinks, not after she ditched me two years ago. But it feels good to have proved her wrong too.

Ten

Neon does a star jump of delight when I tell him that our first class after registration is Music. As soon as we get to Mr Ross's room, he makes a beeline for the guitars, banjos and ukuleles hung up on hooks on the back wall. Neon is one of those people who can pick up an instrument for the first time and know instinctively how to play it – it's the talent I wish I had most in the world.

"Sit down," I whisper. "Mr Ross doesn't like us getting the guitars down without permission."

But Neon can't help himself. He takes a guitar – the nicest one, the one with relatively new strings – from the wall and begins turning the silver pegs to tune it. For a few seconds, everyone stares at him.

Matt Lewis scoffs and rolls his eyes. "Thinks he's Jim Henson, this guy."

Hannah laughs. "I think you mean Jimi Hendrix. Jim Henson's the guy who created the Muppets."

Mr Ross comes in while Neon is tuning the guitar. He's one of my favourite teachers: he's quite young and really into music, but not in a snobby way like Joel and his friends. He's always asking us what we're listening to, and he never looks down on the more commercial stuff. Even so, his eyebrows knit into a frown when he sees a strange kid playing around with one of his guitars.

"This is my friend, Neon," I say, my cheeks flushing. "He's visiting from New York City for a few days."

"Neon?" Mr Ross echoes. I'm starting to wish I'd named the kid Ben or Fraser, something that would blend in better. "Do you play, Neon?"

"Yeah, I'm in a band called The Pyramid Club."

I have another of those dizzying moments when I remember he is my story come to life. I picked that name for his band after reading about a venue in his neighbourhood where loads of famous people performed in the eighties.

Neon strums a chord and looks up at Mr Ross. "Do you mind? I couldn't bring my guitar with me on this trip, so I haven't played in a few days."

"Oh, be my guest." Mr Ross makes a sweeping gesture with his hand. "It's not like I've got a class to teach or anything."

My cheeks burn even hotter, but Neon doesn't pick up on Mr Ross's wry grin or the sarcasm in his voice. Everyone in the class is smirking and muttering. If I was them, I might be too. I hate to say it, but Neon looks so arrogant, waltzing into a classroom, announcing he's in a band, grabbing the spotlight uninvited. But then he starts to play.

He plays a stripped-back acoustic version of an old Kylie Minogue song with a really complicated guitar riff for the bridge – I saw a girl cover it like that online a few years ago and it's still one of my favourites. His voice is light and smooth; his hands move like water over the frets of the guitar.

As he plays, the energy in the room changes. There's something about watching someone this talented doing what they do best. All the cynicism melts away and everyone, even Mr Ross, just enjoys the music, bobbing their heads or half dancing in their seats. It's the best Monday morning I've had in ages.

When Neon finishes, the whole class bursts into applause.

"That was amazing!" Matt shouts. "He actually *is* Jim Henson."

"That was excellent, Neon." Mr Ross looks half impressed, half jealous. He's in a Fall Out Boy cover band called Fall Oot Boy (they sing all the songs in Scots) so he probably has his own dreams of musical stardom. "When did you start to play?"

"Do another one," Hari says, interrupting Neon's story about trying to play his Uncle Mack's guitar with tiny fingers when he was four. Mr Ross tries to protest, saying we need to get on with some work, but half the class boos to drown him out, and eventually he throws up his hands in defeat and says Neon can do *one* more. Just one.

In the end, Neon ends up filling almost two-thirds of the class with songs. He and Mr Ross even do a duet of the only Fall Out Boy song that I (and therefore Neon) actually know. By the time the bell rings, Mr Ross is full-on fanboying over Neon. He even tells him he can take one of the school guitars home to practise with while he's here, which must be a first.

As I'm packing up my stuff, Hari, Russell and Matt rush over to Neon and sweep him out of the classroom without me. Hari says something about a cousin who works for a music label in London, how he could hook him up with some contacts, though Hari once claimed that his uncle was Rihanna's personal driver, and it turned out he only gave her a ride in his taxi. I fall in line beside Caitlin and Hannah.

"Neon is so good!" Caitlin says, slipping her arm through mine. "Like, he could be famous. He probably *will* be famous."

"Maybe." I grin. "Get his autograph while you still can."

"Listen." Hannah links my other arm with hers. "We wanted to say we're sorry that we didn't believe you."

"When I said it sounded too good to be true, I didn't mean Neon was too good *for you*," Caitlin says. "He's not like the boys in our year, you know? He's so interesting and so different. And he's cute."

I give a weak laugh. "It's OK. He kind of is too good to be true."

"Right? I can't believe he was your first kiss. Mine was with *that*." She points across the corridor, where Dylan Jeffries is attempting to fart on one of his friends. He and Caitlin went out for four weeks in first year and she's still embarrassed about it. "You're so lucky, Laurie."

"So." Hannah leans in towards me and lowers her voice. "Have you two kissed again?"

My cheeks burn. Both she and Caitlin sent me multiple messages asking me the same thing yesterday, but I didn't reply.

"No." I glance over at Neon. He's further down the corridor, laughing at something Hari is saying. "Honestly it's not like that at all."

"Laurie!" Caitlin shoves my shoulder playfully. "What are you waiting for? He's leaving on Saturday!"

"He's only been here two days," I say. "Besides it's awkward at my house. Joel's always around."

"Do you want us to get him out of there for you?" Hannah grins. "We could call and tell him that someone's, like, giving out free ice cream at the Co-op. He'd go running out, and you and Neon could have some alone time together."

Caitlin scoffs. "That's so stupid. Joel would recognise our voices for one thing, and he'd wonder why someone had called to tell him personally about free ice cream."

Hannah blinks. Caitlin doesn't often use that sharp, scathing tone with her. It's usually reserved for me.

"I was only joking." Hannah looks down at her hands and picks at her nail polish. "It wasn't a serious suggestion."

"Joel's lactose intolerant, so that wouldn't work." I laugh to clear the atmosphere. "If we told him somebody was giving out free textbooks, it might be different. All he does these days is study."

"So he's not going to barge in on you or anything. Perfect." Caitlin prods me in the arm. "Come on. Go for it before you regret it."

Maybe I actually *should* kiss Neon. The fact that I based his face on mine is pretty weird, but I changed it so much that he looks nothing like me now. That way he really would be my first kiss, like I told Caitlin and Hannah all those months ago. It wouldn't be a lie any more. So many parts of the story that I made up are coming true. Maybe that one should too.

Eleven

Joel makes spaghetti carbonara for tea tonight. It always surprises me when I remember Joel is pretty much an adult now and no longer the Pot Noodle-obsessed teenage boy that I grew up with. He shares a flat with three friends down in St Andrews, and he claims he's the one who does most of the cooking and cleaning. The way Neon goes on about his spaghetti, you'd think we'd invited some Michelin-starred chef over to make dinner for us – the boy is like a personal hype brigade. Joel grins and bats away the compliments, but he's obviously pleased.

Afterwards, Neon offers to take care of dessert, so I wash up while he makes something with eggs and sugar. Joel peers at the bowl as he carries our empty plates to the sink.

"Are you making meringues?"

"A pavlova!" Neon beams. "My grandma's from New Zealand. It comes from there. *Not* Australia," he adds hotly.

I grin – two of Mutti's friends had this argument when they came to visit, and somehow it ended up being part of Neon's story.

Joel sets the plates down on the worktop. "We really don't take dessert that seriously in this house, pal. You don't need to make a whole pavlova," he says. "Doesn't meringue take ages to cook anyway? I've got to get back to my essay."

"No problem. We'll save you some." Neon whisks the eggs and sugar so hard, a bit flies up and lands on his nose. "What are you studying?"

"English Lit."

Joel pulls the tiniest bit of a face. It still seems strange to me that he ended up doing English Literature. He loves reading but at school his favourite subjects were always Drama and Art.

"I'm in my second year. Another two and three-quarters to go."

"What do you want to do afterwards?" Neon asks. "Do you think you'll be a writer like your mom and Laurie?"

"Nah, I don't have their way with words. I really don't know what I'll do, to be honest." Joel nudges me out of the way so he can rinse a cloth under the tap. "Honestly I'm just trying to get my coursework and exams out of the way. I'll think about what comes next when I get to it."

"But what would you do if you could do anything?" Neon puts down the bowl and shakes a cramp out of his right arm. "It doesn't have to be anything to do with your degree. Your dream job."

Joel shrugs. "I always wanted to be an actor, but it's really difficult to get into drama school. Even harder to actually find work."

"He did say *dream* job," I point out, glancing over him as I put the salt and pepper shakers away.

"Exactly. Besides, acting works out for some people," Neon says. "Why don't you go for it?"

Joel falls quiet as he wipes the table. I really think he would make a good actor. He played Tybalt in our school's musical adaptation of *Romeo and Juliet* in his last year, and he stole the show – he was hilarious in the fight scenes. I'm sure our parents would have supported Joel if he'd wanted to go to drama school. Mum used to have a really boring finance job, but she gave it up to buy the bookshop. Mutti doesn't make that much money as an author, but she's never tried to discourage me from becoming a writer like her.

"Nah. It's not for me any more." Joel gives a tight smile. "It's OK to change your mind. You might decide you don't want to be a musician in a few years."

"That's true. I've got a long list of things I want to try out." Neon counts them out on his fingers. "I want to illustrate picture books, and go to culinary school in Paris, and become an international diplomat, and maybe get into social work too."

Joel laughs. "I like your ambition, kid."

"Well –" Neon grins at me as he picks up his bowl of meringue again – "imagination is limitless."

I stay downstairs to hang out with Neon before bed. We watch a couple of episodes of his favourite TV show (also my favourite TV show, unsurprisingly) then play Xbox for a while.

Joel comes downstairs for another cup of coffee after we start. I'm sure he'll want to join in when he sees us playing *Samurai Shodown* – we used to spend hours battling each other on it – but he just tells us not to stay up too late and heads back to his room.

Now that I'm used to the weirdness of Neon being here, I really love having him around. It's been ages since I felt so comfortable with a friend, that I can say what I'm thinking without being judged or laughed at for it. It's like climbing into your favourite pyjamas after a long day in school uniform.

"Can I ask you something?" Neon says. We've paused the game to have a third helping of his (excellent) peach pavlova. "What's the deal with Caitlin and Hannah?"

I take a bite of meringue. "What do you mean?"

"Like, they're pretty funny, and they've been nice to me, but if they really thought I didn't exist, why did they bother coming to the train station on Saturday? It seems like they were trying to embarrass you." Neon pauses, weighing up whether or not to say something. "And at school today so many people said they thought I was made up – that Caitlin *told* them that you made me up. It sounds like she was laughing at you behind your back."

I'm quiet for a long moment, trying to work out how to answer. I think about the time I came home from school in first year and burst into tears because Caitlin had made some snarky comments about my spots. Mutti was ready to march down to her house and give her a piece of her mind, but Mum, who is always more understanding, calmed us both down and reminded me that sometimes people put others down to make themselves feel better about their own insecurities. Whenever Caitlin takes digs at me now, I remind myself that it says more about her than it does about me.

But honestly it doesn't make me feel much better. It's not

nice to have to hear those negative things from someone who's supposed to be a friend. And it's confusing because Caitlin can be so great at other times. I'm never sure where I stand with her. Maybe that's why I liked my made-up conversations with Neon – I always knew where they were going. If we got into a disagreement, I could quickly steer us out of it.

"I think it's just what some people are like," I tell him eventually. "Especially if there are three of you. I see it with other groups in our year too."

I wonder if it's the same with Tilly, Jamie and Elsie. Somehow I don't think so. Whenever I see them in the corridors, they're always laughing, smiling, hugging each other. When there was a Valentine's Day message board set up in the corridor back in February, they all left anonymous messages for each other saying how amazing and gorgeous and brilliant they were – it was easy to tell who they were from because all three of them had drawn *Doctor Who* characters on the notes.

"You deserve friends who are good to you." Neon knocks his knee against mine. "Like the ones you gave me."

The Pyramid Club is made up of four people including Neon. There's Kairo, an unbelievably brilliant drummer who also loves to dance. Yifei, the bassist, possibly the funniest and most sarcastic person in the whole of New York City. And finally Jennie, lead guitarist and backing vocalist, who speaks four languages and makes all her own clothes from scratch. It was fun coming up with people so much more confident than me, who have the talents that I wish I had. But the best part was creating a group of friends who really love each other.

My eyes suddenly feel hot. "Well, I have you now, don't I?"

"Yeah, of course." Neon links his arms round my shoulders and squeezes me tight. "But I'm only here until Saturday. You need other people too."

"Well, Caitlin's been a lot nicer since you got here. Maybe things will be different now."

"I hope so." He scrapes the last of the meringue from his plate and grins at me. "If not, I'll send someone over from the Realm to sort her out. How about the Hulk?"

I laugh and bite into a slice of peach. "You've never seen Caitlin when she's angry. Bruce Banner would be no match for her."

My eyes are still prickly, but there's a warm feeling in my chest too. It's good to know that Neon sees what I see. That someone, even if he may not be fully real, has my back.

Twelve

By lunchtime the next day, word about Neon's performance in Music has spread so far, he's practically a local celebrity. Matt and Hari borrow another guitar at lunch and badger Neon into giving a mini concert in the courtyard. Neon protests at first, but I can tell from his grin that he loves the attention. At first there are only a dozen or so kids from our class watching, but more and more join, teachers and other members of staff too, and soon almost a hundred people have surrounded him. Tilly stands to my left with Jamie Singh and Elsie Jackson. When I catch her eye, she nods.

"He's good," she says. Two words, and it's the most she's spoken to me in two years.

"Thanks," I say. "I mean, I know. He's amazing."

"You guys should perform together. I bet you'd sound great."

My cheeks burn. The thought of singing onstage with an audience absolutely terrifies me. "Nah. I'd probably throw up again."

Tilly is one of the few people who have heard me sing properly. She has a karaoke machine, and we used to spend hours after school and at the weekends performing duets or pretending we were starring in West End musicals. That's the weird thing about ex-best friends – when there's so much you know about each other, you can never go back to being strangers.

Our friendship started to fall apart after we started high school. We were placed in different classes, me in 1C and Tilly in 1D. Tilly became friends with Jamie and Elsie right away. They were into stuff that I knew nothing about – things like manga, *Doctor Who* and Dungeons and Dragons, which Tilly became instantly obsessed with. Soon that was all she talked about, and every second sentence was "Jamie said this" or "Elsie likes that".

When I went to hers one Friday for our usual karaoke session, she criticised every song I suggested – Jamie couldn't stand that band; Elsie thought this singer was so annoying. It made me so angry, I threw the mic across her room.

"Why didn't you invite Elsie and Jamie, then, if they're so much better than me?"

"I wanted to!" Tilly spat back at me. "But my dad said I wasn't allowed to uninvite you, and I didn't want you there with them. You'd spoil everything."

For a moment, all we could do was stare at each other – and then I burst into tears. Tilly went to get me a tissue and gave me a hug, but it felt half-hearted. I was only a couple of centimetres taller and a bit heavier than her, but suddenly I felt huge in her room: a giant soft toy that she'd long outgrown and was only now getting around to throwing away.

"Sorry. I really didn't mean to upset you. And you wouldn't spoil anything. That was a really mean thing to say." She looked down at her wrist and tugged at the friendship bracelet that I made for her at Brownies when we were eight. "I just feel like we're growing apart a bit. I can't help it."

By then, I was already friendly with Caitlin and Hannah, so on Monday I moved to their table at lunch. And that was it. There was no Friendship Over announcement, no angry messages sent to or received on our phones. One day, I noticed Tilly had taken the bracelet off, so I took mine off too. I didn't speak to her again.

The way we act now, it's like we barely knew each other at all. Sometimes I feel like I really don't know her any more, like when she'd signed up for the ski trip next month. She always hated sports and PE, so I never would have guessed she'd want to try something like that. I was surprised when I heard she'd come out as pansexual too. Not in a bad way – I have two mums so obviously it's not an issue for me. I just didn't see it coming.

I glance over at Neon, who's now playing an acoustic version of a Beyoncé song – Caitlin and Hannah are swaying and waving the torches on their phones like they're at a concert. If Neon feels nervous, it doesn't show. His smile grows with the crowd, warm and inviting. When I look back at Tilly, she's laughing about something with Jamie. I've already been forgotten.

By the time the bell rings, Neon's voice is starting to go hoarse and he's shaking the cramp out of his fingers. I go to join him as the crowd disperses, Caitlin and Hannah right behind me.

"Sorry about that." For the first time, he looks quite sheepish. "I didn't mean to put on a mini concert. I just love playing so much."

I grin at him. "That's OK. I'm surprised you're still talking to us, now you're famous."

He mimes putting sunglasses on. "Well, I need a crew. Know any tour managers?"

"I can do it. You'll see the world." I spread my hands in an arc through the air. "Inverness! Nairn! Drumnadrochit!"

"I don't know where most of those places are, but they sound extremely glamorous." He swings his arm round my shoulders. "You can't be my manager, though. You'll be too busy performing with me."

"What do you mean, performing?" Hannah stops walking and grabs my arm. "Laurie Rebecca Storey-Peters. Can you sing?"

I instantly wish the ground would swallow me up. "Nah, not really."

"Lies!" Neon shouts. "She's really good. *Way* better than me. Like, not quite Adele level or anything, but definitely good enough to be one of Adele's backing singers."

Beside me, Caitlin's face has fallen. "Are you serious? Why didn't you tell us?"

When we first became friends, Caitlin and Hannah had already joined their musical-theatre class in Inverness and they talked about it a *lot*. It was their thing, their identity. I felt as if there was no space for me to like singing too. It's always that way with Caitlin, even with little things. Her favourite animal is the platypus, which was always *my* favourite, but when I excitedly told her back in first year she looked so annoyed that I never brought it up again.

I shrug awkwardly. "It's not a big deal. I basically only sing in the shower. The thought of performing in front of anyone who's not my family is terrifying."

Hannah claps her hands. "Ooh, you should sing together at Friday Showcase!"

Once a month, our school does something called Friday Showcase. It's usually filled with the school choir, the Highland-dancing group and this fourth-year boy who's a cello prodigy, but anyone can perform if they want to. Caitlin and Hannah have done it a couple of times. All you need do is add your name to the sign-up sheet at reception.

Once Hannah has explained what it is to Neon, his face lights up. "Let's do it! That's my last day. It would be the perfect way to say goodbye."

"But Laurie's so shy," Caitlin says. "I really can't see her doing that."

For once, I don't think Caitlin is trying to be mean. She's actually trying to stop me from being pushed into something that I don't want to do. But I'm so used to her criticising me that it makes me defensive. She doesn't get to decide what I can and can't do, what I can and can't be.

"Maybe I will," I say hotly. "Wait and see."

Thirteen

I might be biased, but I genuinely think Every Book & Cranny is one of the best bookshops on the planet. The building used to be a church and lots of the features are still there: the domed roof, a few stained-glass windows, a wooden pulpit that my parents fitted with comfy seating so people can relax and read. They have all the big names and bestsellers, but they also stock loads of books by little-known authors or indie publishers and translations from all over the world. It might not bring in as many customers as bigger shops, but those it does have are very loyal – a few make the trip up here from different parts of the country every year to see Mum's latest additions to the shelves.

Neon and I head to the shop after school on Tuesday. I've been putting off taking him there – it feels like Mum or Mutti could jump out from behind a bookcase at any moment, even though I know they're currently miles away. But Neon's desperate to see it, and deep down I want to show it off too.

Gio is standing behind the counter when we come in. Hearing the bell on the door jingle, he looks up and gives us a big wave. "My favourite co-worker! Don't tell your brother I said that."

"Hey, Gio." It's been a while since I saw him and the sight of his shiny bald head and twirly moustache makes me smile. "How's business?"

"A bit slow. We had a good group of people in at lunchtime, but hardly anyone since then. I sent Joel home at three. No point in us both being here, and it sounds like he's busy with uni work." He smiles at Neon. "I don't think I know your friend."

"This is Neon," I say. "He's from New York. Neon, this is Gio."

Gio is from Bergamo in Italy. He wandered into the shop while he was on holiday in Scotland six years ago, saw the ad looking for a general manager that Mum had posted up on the corkboard by the door, and ended up uprooting his whole life to stay and run the place. He's like an uncle to me and Joel now. He comes over for dinner once a fortnight, and he spent a few Christmases with us during the pandemic, when he wasn't able to go back to Italy.

"Neon! What an interesting name." Gio holds out his hand to shake Neon's. It seems Joel hasn't told him about our visitor, which is a relief – Gio is great but he would definitely report back to Mum and Mutti if he knew there was a strange boy staying at our house. "So you've moved over here?"

"Uh, no, I'm only visiting. Heading home on Saturday." Neon smiles. "I really like it here, though! Everyone's so friendly, and I love how green everything is. I wish I could stay longer."

Gio smiles. "I know what you mean. This place drew me in too, and it hasn't let me go yet."

A customer comes in then and asks Gio about a thriller that's due to be published next week, so Neon and I go wandering through the bookcases. We have three shelves dedicated to staff recommendations, and there are a few of my cards up: the first part of a Norwegian fantasy trilogy, three graphic novels and a YA book about a boy band who are secretly sea monsters.

"Have you met characters from any of these?" I whisper to Neon, glancing at Gio to make sure he's still busy. "They're all in the Realm, right?"

"Yeah, of course. I recognise a few of them."

Neon reaches for a copy of *Shadows of the Sea*, the YA novel. Tilly is always posting about it online, so I eventually read it a few months ago. I liked it so much that I had to write a card for it.

"Callan and I hang out sometimes," he says, tapping the picture of a boy with bright blue skin on the front cover.

"No way!" I instantly wish I could tell Tilly. She'd lose her mind. "But he's so awful!"

Neon laughs. "He is but he's hilarious too."

"Who else?" I ask excitedly. "Anyone famous?"

"Loads of people. The March sisters, Miles Morales, Garfield... About a dozen different versions of Sherlock Holmes," he adds, pointing to a copy of *The Hound of the Baskervilles* as we arrive at the classics section. "Those famous characters are the ones who stand out most in the Realm. The others all disappear eventually."

"Disappear? What do you mean?"

"It's just what happens there." Neon shrugs and picks

up an illustrated edition of *Pride and Prejudice*. "Some characters stick around forever, especially popular and well-known ones, but the rest fade away after a while. If everyone in the real world forgets about them, they get weaker and weaker, and then they dissolve into nothing."

Neon says this matter-of-factly, but his words are steeped in sadness. I wonder how many friends he's lost this way. Maybe even characters that I made up when I started writing his story – it was a while ago now, and I don't remember all the friends and relatives that I featured in those complicated first few chapters.

Two older customers come in then, so Gio sends them to me for help while he searches the shelves with the thriller man. The couple are looking for a picture book for their granddaughter, so I take them to the kids' section and talk them through some of my favourites. They choose a story about bunnies wreaking havoc on public transport and take it up to the till, which makes me happy – sometimes I spend ages talking through new books with customers and then they turn round and say they'll buy them cheaper online.

When I come back, Neon is standing at the window. I tell him about my sale to the grandparents, but he doesn't reply; when I call his name, he doesn't even seem to hear me. Eventually he looks round, his face pale.

"What's wrong?" I ask.

"I … thought I saw something weird."

"What?"

I look through the window. The café across the road is closing up for the day, and two dog walkers have stopped to have a chat while their animals sniff round a lamp post.

Nothing unusual.

"Just something – someone I thought I knew." Neon gives a quick shake of his head. "Come on, show me the rest of the shop. I haven't even seen the cookbooks yet."

～

We hang out in Every Book & Cranny so long, the street is dark and the shops are closing by the time we leave. Martha is coming out of Bohemian Catsody as we walk past. Neon waves to say hi, then sings the Queen song that the shop was named after all the way to our house. A few people stare but I don't mind too much. I even join in with the chorus, though not as loudly as him.

"You really are good, you know," Neon says when we reach the end of the song. "We should definitely do that Friday Showcase thing together."

"I don't know…" The burst of bravery I felt back at school has faded now. "I get really bad stage fright. When I was six, I was one of the Three Wise Men in our school nativity play, and I got so nervous I threw up in Russell's hair."

Neon laughs. "I'll stand a couple of metres away from you just in case. But lots of musicians and performers get really nervous, you know. It's all about practice."

We turn the corner on to our road and walk down the long line of houses with glowing windows and cars in the driveways. In the light from our kitchen, I see a red-headed figure standing on the front doorstep: Carrie.

I spin round and shake my head at Neon. "*Hide!*"

"What?" He blinks. "Where?"

"I don't know! In the bushes or something!"

Neon flaps his arms in a panic but dives into the bush beside us as Carrie turns round. There's a Pyrex dish in her hands and a sparkle in her eye. I know that look – it's her gossip glint, the expression she gets when there's a juicy bit of gen to be sniffed out.

"Hello, lovely. I thought I'd pop over and see how you're getting on." She moves down from the step as I walk up the path to our house. "Everything OK?"

"All good!" I take out my keys and squeeze past Carrie to unlock the front door. "Haven't burned the house down yet."

"So I see. Well done." Carrie cranes to the left to peer into the hallway. "Is it just you and Joel in there? Only I noticed a boy coming home with you after school yesterday, and I don't think I saw him leave."

Oh no. I swallow and put on what I hope is a confused frown. "Oh yeah, that was my friend from school. He definitely went home, though! Unless he's hiding in the bushes or something."

I laugh, probably too loudly, and silently pray that Neon doesn't choose this exact moment to cough, sneeze or get attacked by bugs and come rolling on to the pavement.

Carrie smiles and leans against the wall. "Laurie, I know it must be quite fun having the house to yourselves, but I don't think Liv and Monika would be very happy if they knew you were having boys staying over."

My cheeks go hot. "It's really not like that! He's my friend. Nothing else."

I don't know how many times I've said that since Neon arrived. Why do some people have trouble believing a boy and girl can be friends and nothing else? Apart from being annoying, it seems a bit rude to assume we're both straight.

"Honestly, Carrie, he definitely went home. It was quite late, though. We were working on something for school."

"Oh yeah? What's that, then?"

I should have known Carrie 'Nancy Drew' O'Connor would ask for details. "A song. We're going to perform it together at school on Friday."

"Oh, brilliant! I've heard you singing at home a few times. You sound great." She finally hands over the dish in her hands, as if it's a reward for providing her with some vaguely interesting information. "Anyway – shepherd's pie. My veggie version. I thought you and Joel could have it for your tea. I noticed you had a delivery on Saturday night, so I figured you'd used up that takeaway money already!"

She laughs, waves and heads back to her house. Neon has the good sense to wait until she's safely inside before emerging from the bush. He scurries down the path and hurries through my front door. His eyes are bright.

"So we're doing it? We're actually going to sing together?"

"No!" I close the door and pick a leaf out of Neon's hair. "That was the first thing that came into my head."

"Oh, come *onnnn*." Neon drags the word all the way to the kitchen. "What if Carrie mentions it in front of your moms?"

"Then I'll lie again," I say, though the thought of that makes me feel uncomfortable.

I'm a good liar because I have a good memory. When I was making up my story about Neon for Caitlin and Hannah, I had to keep track of everything I'd said so I didn't contradict myself. But I've had to tell so many lies recently. I don't want to add any more to the list unless it's totally necessary.

"Come on, Laurie," Neon whines again. He puts his hands on my shoulders and pouts. "I'll have to go back to the Realm on Saturday, so if you think about it this is my *dying wish*. Don't you want to grant a fictional character their dying wish?"

"You're not dying." I laugh and push him away, but his pout doesn't fade. I sigh and throw my hands up. "Fine, I'll do it! Don't blame me if I throw up on your hair."

Fourteen

Neon signs us up for Friday Showcase as soon as we get to school the next day. He even writes our names in pink highlighter and capital letters to be extra annoying. We spend the whole of double Art debating which song to sing. Lots of things about Neon are the exact opposite of me – the things I want to be but am not, the parts of me I want to change but can't – but we have the exact same taste in music: film soundtracks, girl groups and big power ballads. Even so, it's not easy to find a song that fits his voice and mine and isn't some cheesy love song.

"How about something from a musical?" Hannah suggests, glancing up from her painting. "Ooh, you could do 'Suddenly Seymour' from *Little Shop of Horrors*!"

"That's a full-on love song, Hannah. Exactly what they said they didn't want." Caitlin rolls her eyes. "Besides, not everyone is as into musicals as you."

Hannah stares at her. "You love musicals too. We go to the same musical-theatre class!"

"Yeah, but you're, like, *obsessed* with them. It's kind of weird."

Hurt flashes over Hannah's face as she dips her paintbrush

into water. Caitlin has been different with her the past couple of days. Different with me as well. She's been linking her arm with mine more than usual, and when she had to pick teams for football in PE yesterday she chose me before Hannah. It's as if having Neon here has shifted the dynamic between us. Because of him, Caitlin sees me as someone capable of having a friend like Neon – someone who could *kiss* a boy like Neon. In Caitlin's mind, there's always a hierarchy, and I've been bumped up a spot.

Honestly some part of me is happy about that. I've felt like the odd one out in our trio for so long, it's nice to find myself in second place. But, at the same time, I feel bad for Hannah – I know what it's like to have Caitlin pick at your sentences, digging around for something she can use to make fun of you.

Neon looks up from his painting to frown at her. "That's not weird. I love musicals."

He belts out something from *Les Misérables* so loudly that Matt Lewis jumps and knocks his paint over. Neon rushes over to help him, still singing as he does so. Hannah joins in, the hurt from Caitlin's comments melting away as she gets into the song. A few more people start singing along, me included. Mrs Watson tells everyone to settle down and get on with their work, but then even she joins in with the chorus. It feels like a scene from a film – something that never would have happened before Neon arrived.

"I saw *Les Mis* on Broadway a few years ago," he says, once the impromptu rendition is finally over. "I had the soundtrack on repeat for a month. Drove my mom crazy."

"You did?" I say. "I didn't know that."

That's not something that I made up about him. Neon must be embellishing his own history. That makes me a bit nervous – if our stories don't match, people are going to be suspicious. Then again, no one knows every single little thing about their friends or anyone else. It's normal that there are huge parts of Neon's past that I don't know about.

A while later, Neon runs out of green paint for his forest landscape. He goes to the supplies cupboard to get more, and Caitlin scoots along to sit beside me.

"How's Operation Kiss the Boy going?" she whispers.

I shake my head rapidly, my eyes fixed on my painting of Ben Nevis. "It's not. I told you, we're friends."

"Laurie! Come on." Caitlin tugs at my sleeve. "You've only got a few days left!"

"We don't want you to regret it after he leaves," Hannah says, leaning over the desk towards me. "Who knows when you might see him again?"

Caitlin starts chanting, 'Kiss him, kiss him,' in a low voice, though not so low that no one else can hear – Russell turns round from the desk in front of us with a big grin on his face. Neon comes back to the table with the paint, so Caitlin hops back to her own stool, and Hannah sits up with a smile, waggling her eyebrows at me before looking back down at her painting.

While Neon pours the paint into his plastic tray, I take a long look at him: the birthmark over his eyebrow, the dark hair curling behind his ears. I still don't know if I actually want to kiss him. I've been thinking about it a lot, but whenever we're alone, and I have the chance, I remember that he's a fictional character that I made up, and it gets too weird. Even if he was as normal as any other boy, I'm not sure if I like him like that.

"Hey, how about you sing 'Don't Stop Believin'"?" Hannah says. "There's this version I've seen online for a boy and a girl, from that show *Glee*. It's not a love song. It's about believing in yourself and your dreams."

"Oh, I love that song!" Neon sings the first few lines. "What do you think, Laurie?"

It's a fitting title for our story, our friendship. I've never seen the show, but I've heard the version of the song that Hannah is talking about and I like it. I think it would suit our voices.

"I'm not sure I can hit those high notes." I dab at my painting and try to ignore the nerves writhing in my stomach. "But we can give it a go. It's our best option so far."

"Trust you to suggest something from *Glee*, Hannah." Caitlin snorts and shakes her head. I raise my eyebrows at her and she lifts her hands in self-defence. "It's a good idea, though. What are you called, by the way? You need a band name."

We all throw out a few suggestions. Russell, Hari and some others overhear us talking and join in too. They have lots of ideas but they all sound too dark and rocky for who we are and the type of songs we plan to sing.

"It's got to be Neon something," Hari says. "I know that makes it seem like you're the lead singer, but it's too good a name not to use."

"Neon something..." Neon taps his mouth with his paintbrush and looks around the room for inspiration. "Neon Paint Pot?"

Hannah laughs at that. "Neon Easel?"

"Neon Superglue." Russell sweeps a streak of orange paint across his sunset. "Or how about Neon Story? That way it sounds like Laurie's surname too. The first half of it anyway."

Neon and I look at each other, and we both know that's the one. Neon Story. It sounds sparkly, glitzy, like the words should be written in glowsticks. And, for reasons we can't explain to Russell and the others, it suits our situation perfectly.

Picking a song and a name somehow makes the fact we're going to perform at Friday Showcase finally seem real. Twenty minutes later, a rush of nerves so strong it makes me feel physically sick comes over me. None of my friends would get it – Caitlin and Hannah have done lots of shows with their theatre group, and Neon was practically born performing – so I ask to go to the toilet and hide in a cubicle while I try to calm down. I can already feel all those eyes in the audience staring at me. Judging me. Waiting for me to mess up.

A few minutes later, the door opens with a squeak and footsteps cross the space. Somehow I know they belong to Tilly Chan. There's something about the way she walks: one slow step then another slightly faster one, like her right foot is trying to keep up with her left. I wait until she goes into a stall before I leave to wash my hands so we don't cross paths, but she comes out a few seconds later holding a piece of toilet paper. Our eyes meet in the mirror. Our faces freeze, then we both push our mouths into something like smiles.

"Oh. Hey." Tilly blows her nose on the paper. "Again."

"Hi." It's funny that we didn't speak a single word to each other for so long, and now that Neon's here we've talked twice in one week. "Is your hay fever bad again?"

"No, I think I'm getting a cold." Tilly tosses the paper into the bin under the sink. There's a pin on her jacket – a rainbow flag. I've never noticed that before. "I saw you and Neon signed up for Friday Showcase."

"Oh yeah. We did," I say, shaking my hands dry. "It's just one song."

It always makes me sad how awkward I feel around Tilly now. Outside my family, she was the person I felt most comfortable with, who made me laugh more than anyone else in the world. When we stopped talking, it felt like turning a dimmer switch on my own personality. There were so many times I'd have a strange thought or a funny idea, something only she would get, but nowhere to put it without her.

"That's great." She takes a couple of steps towards the door. "I didn't think you had it in you."

In a flash, the sadness transforms into anger. "How would you know what I do and don't have in me? You never talk to me any more."

Tilly turns to me with wide eyes. Her hand is clutching the door handle, but she doesn't open it. "What are you talking about? You're the one who stopped talking to me."

"Because you said you didn't want to be friends any more!"

"I didn't say that." Her cheeks are going red. "I said we were growing apart. It was obviously going to happen eventually. You made friends with the popular girls.

You totally looked down on Jamie and Elsie."

"No, I didn't!" My voice bounces off the bathroom walls. "You looked down on me because I didn't know about Dragons and Dungeons or whatever. All of a sudden, you had this whole new life with new friends and new interests, and I was so boring and immature for not knowing anything about it."

"It's Dungeons and Dragons." (I knew that. I also knew it would annoy her if I got it wrong.) "You could have asked about it. I asked you if you wanted to play one time, remember?"

I scoff. "Yeah, but probably only because your dad made you."

Tilly's cheeks flare again. "I shouldn't have said that. It was the truth but I shouldn't have said it."

"Whatever. It was ages ago."

I shrug, like it's nothing, but a crack forms in my anger and some sadness seeps back in. I've spent loads of time imagining what I would say to Tilly if we ever spoke again. It usually ended with us both admitting that we missed each other and vowing to be friends again. Not like this.

The silence stretches between us. There's a moment where I could be the one to take the first step, to say that I'm sorry and that I miss her. But I don't. The door swings open, almost knocking Tilly over, and a flock of noisy first-year girls pours into the bathroom, trampling all over our moment.

"You're right. It was ages ago." Tilly pushes her hair behind her ears and gives a smile that's not really a smile. "Good luck for Friday."

Fifteen

Neon and I spend the whole of the next evening practising our song for the showcase with the guitar Neon borrowed from Mr Ross. I've never sung with someone like this before, and I'm surprised by how good it feels: there's something so satisfying about our voices rising and falling in perfect unison, like birds twirling round each other in a cloudless sky. When it's the two of us in my living room, I don't think about tomorrow's audience or what they might think of me. It's just me and Neon, in our own little world.

"You sound amazing," he says. "I don't get how you don't hear it."

"It's not the singing part that worries me." I flop on to the sofa with a sigh. "It's having to do it with dozens of people watching."

"Imagine we're playing with my band. Pretend you're Yifei or Jennie! They've got tons of confidence. I bet you could feel like that too."

The way I wrote them, Yifei looks like a model and Jennie has enough stage presence to fill a dozen stadiums all by herself. I laugh at the idea that I could be anything like them, but Neon's face stays serious.

"I'm not kidding, Laurie! You created us. It must be in you somewhere."

I start to tell him that I don't think it works like that, but then Joel comes into the living room. He has his laptop under one arm, a huge textbook under the other and a giant cup of tea in his hands.

"You two sound really good." Joel sets his mug down on the coffee table and drops into the armchair. "If you're looking for more male-female duets, there's this great jungle-pop duo I like. They sing in Portuguese, though, so that might be a bit tricky."

I try *really* hard to suppress an eyeroll but fail. Neon smiles.

"Thanks. It's probably time we took a break. We want to be in peak condition for tomorrow." He leans his guitar against the wall, sits down beside me and props his feet up on the table. "What's your essay about?"

"*The Death of the Author*. It's this essay by a critic called Roland Barthes." Joel pulls the textbook on to his lap, flicking the corners of the pages with one finger. "It basically says that when you're reading, you shouldn't focus on what the writer was trying to say or who they were. It should be all about the story itself, however the reader interprets it. What the author meant to do doesn't really matter."

The idea gets me thinking about Neon. He's exactly the way I wrote him, but maybe that will change the more people he interacts with. I like the idea. I want him to be his own person, not a character that I created.

Neon clearly finds the theory interesting too. He points

out that an author's background influences a story in major ways – someone who has had a certain experience or come from a certain place or culture is going to write about it differently to someone who hasn't, and usually more accurately.

But Joel looks bored talking about it, so I change the subject. "How was the shop today? Still quiet?"

"Way too quiet. We only had about four people in all afternoon." His eyebrows knit as he takes a long sip from his tea. "Gio seemed pretty down. I think he's worried about sales."

My heart sinks. "Maybe Mum will come back from London with some ideas. You know she's going to visit every bookshop she comes across."

As if our parents heard us, my phone begins to ring and Mutti's name appears on the screen. Neon shoots me a panicked glance, then leaps over the back of the sofa to hide. I press the green button, and, after a moment, Mutti's face appears in front of a plain white wall with a grainy print of a London bus.

"Hi, ducky!" Mutti grins and waves at me. "So sorry we haven't called sooner – we've been really busy."

"That's OK. How's it all going?"

Mutti fills me in on the events that she's done – including one where a very famous author annoyed everyone by eating an entire tray of mini quiches – then passes the phone to Mum, who shows me the books she picked up at her favourite London shops. They ask about school, how Joel's uni work is going and how things have been in the shop. Joel gives vague answers, not wanting to spoil their trip by telling them how quiet it's been, and they don't push him for details.

While Joel's talking, Neon sticks his head out from behind the sofa like a whale surfacing for air. I widen my eyes to tell him to stay hidden. The camera on my phone is facing away from him, but even having him in my sight feels risky. I'm sure Joel will tell them that I've made a new friend, just to make me sweat, but he's talking to Mum about his essay and doesn't mention it. When he hands the phone back to me, I give a nervous smile and tell my parents I need to go and do my French homework.

"OK, love. Good plan." Mum blows me a kiss then tilts the phone towards Mutti, who looks up from the coffee machine to wave goodbye. "See you on Saturday."

After the call, Joel goes upstairs to continue working on his essay, and Neon and I run through 'Don't Stop Believin'' again. Halfway through the second chorus, he suddenly breaks off. His face freezes, his eyes fixed on something outside the window. I turn round: the street is deserted apart from a woman walking with a little girl of around three years old.

"What's wrong?" I ask.

"Nothing…" He blinks rapidly. "I thought I saw something out there."

"That's what you said in the bookshop the other day! What's going on?"

Neon insists it's nothing, but I keep pushing until he eventually gives in. He walks into the hallway and pulls open the front door, flooding the house with cool air. When I open my mouth to ask what he's doing, he shushes me and points across the street. The woman has stopped to retie the kid's shoelaces outside number eight.

"There," Neon says, pointing to the wheelie bins to their left. "Do you see that?"

The woman takes the little girl in her arms and carries on walking. A moment later, something appears from behind the bins: a baby-pink bunny wearing a white woolly hat. It looks around shiftily, then darts up the street and hides behind a parked car. The rabbit takes another nervous glance around, then hurries on to catch up with the woman and child. The little girl waves over her grown-up's shoulder, beaming. When the woman turns into a house on the corner, the bunny hops over the hedge and leaps into the garden.

It's another thirty seconds or so before I can find my voice again. "What ... was that?"

"I think it's an imaginary friend." Neon scratches his eyebrow. "I saw it on Tuesday too. I don't understand how it got here."

"Probably the same way you did, right?" I say, keeping my voice to a whisper so Carrie doesn't hear. "If the wee girl believes in it that strongly, then..."

"Yeah, but there are *loads* of kids who believe in their imaginary friends. It's really, really uncommon for anyone to cross over into the real world, so it's strange there are two of us in exactly the same place."

Neon is quiet for a moment, a rare frown on his face. I almost don't recognise him when he looks like that. In the photos that I made of him, he was always smiling. Always happy.

"Are you OK?" I put my hand on his arm. "Is it a bad sign that something else from the Realm has ended up here?"

"I don't know. Maybe." Neon shrugs and replaces the frown with a too-bright smile. "It's probably a coincidence. The bunny will find its way back soon enough. Come on – let's go through the song one more time."

Sixteen

Friday Showcase takes place in the afternoon, which means I have half a day to suffer through before Neon and I get up onstage. I'm so nervous that I can't pay attention in class, can't eat anything, can only half listen when Caitlin and Hannah talk to me. As soon as the bell rings at the end of lunch, I pull Neon to one side of the canteen.

"I can't do it. I'm sorry, I just can't." I wrap my arms round myself, shivering in the cold air. "You'll be OK to perform by yourself, right? We can say I have a headache or something."

"No! Laurie, you *can* do this." Neon puts both hands on my shoulders and leans down slightly, looking at me square in the eye like I'm a boxer about to go into the ring. "We've practised the song a thousand times. You'll be perfect!"

"But what if I mess up?"

The idea of all those faces looking at me while I stumble over the verses, even pointing and laughing at me... It makes me want to run home and hide under my bed for the rest of the week.

"Then I'll mess up even worse, and you'll look great by comparison." Neon throws his hands into the air.

99

"Even if we do make a mistake, so what? What's the worst that could happen?"

Caitlin's face floats into my mind. I've seen her sneer at so many people, me included. She's been nicer to me since Neon came, but he's leaving tomorrow. What if everything goes back to normal once he's gone?

"Look, if you really don't want to, I'm not going to force you." Neon tilts his head to the side and narrows his eyes. He has a way of looking at me that feels like he's scanning my soul. "But I think you *do* want to. I think you created me as this big, loud personality who will perform at the drop of a hat because part of you wants to be like that too. Maybe not to the same extent as me – I know I'm a bit much sometimes."

I laugh and follow him into the corridor. "You're not too much, Neon. You're exactly right."

Since Neon and I signed up late, we're performing last, which means I have another agonising thirty-minute wait before we get to go up onstage. I'm so anxious, I almost forget to clap after Mikey the cello prodigy's Vivaldi piece. After an eternity, Mr Ross arrives at the end of the list.

"Finally, we've got Laurie Storey-Peters and her friend Neon, who is visiting from New York this week." He scans the audience to find us. "Come on up, you two."

Neon grabs my hand and pulls me up before I can chicken out. Mr Ross helps us carry a couple of microphones to the middle of the stage. My hands shake as I turn mine on. Neon taps his to test it and makes a loud squealing sound. Everyone winces, then laughs when Neon apologises to the microphone. He turns to the audience and smiles, looking like a total pro.

"Hi. Thanks a lot for having us. I've really liked being part of your school this week. I wish I could stay longer." Someone from the crowd – Hari, I think – gives a whoop of agreement, and Neon grins. "Oh, and we have a band name too! It's Neon Story, and this is 'Don't Stop Believin'."

He starts to play the familiar opening bars on his guitar. My pulse races faster as I look out at the audience. A few people are smiling; some look bored; some are whispering to their friends. Out of everyone there, it's Tilly's eye that catches mine. She quickly glances away, and I look down at the microphone. My hands are clammy and my mouth has gone so dry, I don't know if I'll even be able to sing.

Neon belts out the first few lines. His voice is low to begin with, but bright and clear, every note in the right place. Suddenly it seems so silly that I'm up here with him, sharing his spotlight. I'm not like him, all charming and charismatic. I'm not a performer. That's why I made him the way he is, why I gave him a name that stands out and shines – because it gave me a way to be someone I'm not. Someone I'll never be.

And suddenly I'm sure that everyone else can see it too. When the song reaches my verse, all I do is shake my head.

"Sorry," I whisper. "I can't. I can't."

Neon's hand slips on the guitar strings. Hundreds of eyes follow me as I hurry off the stage and across the hall. Hannah and Caitlin both sit up in their seats in the first row. Hannah looks worried; Caitlin has the tiniest hint of a smile on her face, but she wipes it away as I sweep past. Neon shouts after me, but I pretend not to hear.

"Sorry, folks. Laurie's not feeling well, so it looks like I've gone solo!" He forces a laugh. A few people join in.

"So, uh… How about a bit of Harry Styles instead?"

There's a light smattering of applause as I push open the door to the hall. I don't stick around to watch Neon perform, even when he announces he's going to do one of my favourite songs. Tears are pushing at the back of my eyes, hot and prickly. I'm so angry at myself, but not for running away. I'm angry that I ever thought I could do this in the first place.

The courtyard is deserted since everyone is at the showcase, but I only have a short moment of peace – we get to go home early on Fridays, so after a few minutes the bell rings and people pour out through the doors. A few stare at me as they go past. Some give me sympathetic smiles, but most don't seem surprised that I croaked.

I wait for Neon by the gates and hope that he'll come out alone, not with Caitlin or Hannah or anyone else. As if he's read my mind, a minute later he comes sprinting through the doors like he's trying to outrun them all.

"I'm sorry," I blurt out, shaking my head. "I couldn't do it."

Neon swings an arm round me and pulls me into a hug. "Don't worry about it. Let's just go home."

We hurry away from school before Caitlin and the others can catch up with us. My phone begins to buzz in my pocket, probably with messages from her and Hannah. I don't read them right away. They might be genuinely nice but they might not be, and that would make me feel even worse.

"So what happened?" Neon asks once we're nearly at my house. "Stage fright?"

I explain as best as I can. Now that the showcase is over

and we're away from school, my reaction seems quite silly. Even if I'd been really, really bad, it's not like people were going to shout and throw tomatoes at us. Caitlin might have made a few mean comments, but she and everyone else would have forgotten about it eventually. But it was like my body went into flight mode: all I wanted to do was get out of there.

"Sorry," I say again. "It would have been awesome to do something like that together. That was our only chance to sing together before you leave, and I ruined it."

"Well, actually…" Neon pauses on the corner to the next street. "You don't need to worry about that because I've made a decision."

"Yeah?" I look at him. "What decision?"

Neon takes a long look around, surveying the rows of houses, the gardens with washing hanging up to dry or bikes lying on the grass – this quiet, uneventful slice of reality. Then he leans in and whispers something to me with a wide grin on his face.

"I'm not going back."

Seventeen

"What do you mean, you're not going back?"

We're in the kitchen at my house. Joel is out, probably doing his shift at the bookshop, but I keep my voice low – I wouldn't put it past Carrie to be listening in with a glass pressed against the wall. She was washing her bright yellow Beetle in her driveway when we got back, so Neon had to climb over the garden wall and sneak in through the back door while I distracted her by asking about a reality show that she's obsessed with.

"I don't want to," Neon says now. "I'm going to stay here. In the real world. With you."

He drops a piece of bread into the toaster as casually as if this was his home. For a moment, I imagine a reality where it actually is his home: where he keeps sleeping on our sofa bed and coming to school with me, and somehow my parents are fine with it. That's beyond even *my* imagination.

"But you said you'd get in trouble for leaving – won't people there notice you're gone?" I ask. "Besides, the Realm sounds amazing! There are so many mythical or imaginary creatures that we don't have here, and you get to meet famous characters, and…"

"Yeah, but it turns out I like being real. I like eating real food. I like breathing real air. I feel more solid here. More like myself and not … whatever I was before. A figment of your imagination, I guess." Neon reaches into the cupboard for the peanut butter. "They'll be mad, sure, but I think they'll let it go eventually. I'm just one character, and I look human – it's not like they've got King Kong on the loose."

"But what about your mum?" I ask. "And Cauliflower and the band and everyone?"

A flash of sadness crosses Neon's face. "I'll miss them. Of course I will. But remember what I told you, about how characters in the Realm fade away when people forget about them? That'll happen to them eventually." He's quiet for a moment, his fingers tapping against the worktop as he waits for the toaster to ping. "It'll happen to me too."

"Neon, I could never forget you." I give a shaky laugh. "Are you joking? Do you really think I could forget about the time my imaginary best friend actually came to visit?"

"OK, maybe not me," he says, "but you *will* forget about the others. In a few years, you'll move away and meet new people and have a new life, and all of this will be a memory – a story you told yourself long ago. You'll think about me from time to time, but you won't be able to tell anyone else in your life what happened because they won't believe you. Everyone I love will disappear, and I'll become more and more faded until eventually I'm almost nothing."

A heavy silence stretches between us. Outside a robin sings a wistful tune.

"I don't want that. I don't want you to disappear," I say quietly. "But it's more complicated than what we want, Neon. Where are you going to live, for one thing? You can't sleep on our sofa bed forever."

"We'll figure something out." He catches his toast as it pops up. "Maybe your parents will have some ideas."

The thought of telling Mutti and Mum is a definite nope for me. There is absolutely no chance they would believe Neon's story about coming from a realm of fictional creations – and, to be fair, 99.9 per cent of people on Earth wouldn't, either. My parents' first step would be to get in touch with Neon's mum, and when they realised she didn't seem to exist they'd have a million more questions about who this boy was and how he got here. Social services would have to get involved, maybe even the police. They'd eventually realise that there was no record of Neon existing anywhere, and the whole thing would be a total mess, and I'd be in a ton of trouble.

"No," I say. "Sorry. There's no way we can tell them."

"Well, we'll have to find another place, then. The world is huge! There must be somewhere I can stay."

He says this quite cheerfully as he spreads peanut butter on his toast. I don't think he realises how complicated all this is. He might be fourteen in the Realm, but he's brand new to reality.

There's about a hundred and thirty pounds in my savings account. I'm not sure how much the B&Bs around here cost, but that wouldn't get us more than a few nights. A hostel would be cheaper, but the nearest one is in Inverness, and I wouldn't want to send him all the way there by himself.

There are so many thoughts whirling round my head that I don't realise I've been silent for almost a minute. Neon's smile is starting to fade. "Don't you want me to stay, Laurie?"

"Of course I do," I say quickly, and I really mean it. "But it's complicated."

I run through everyone I know, trying to find someone who might be able to help us. Hannah is one of four siblings – there's never any room at her house. Caitlin just lives with her mum now her sister's moved out, but their place is tiny. My grandparents on Mutti's side are back in Germany, my granny on Mum's side is in a care home, and none of my aunts or uncles live within a hundred miles of us. Gio has a spare room at his place, but he'd definitely tell my parents if I asked.

Then it comes to me. "I know! Tilly's house!"

Tilly's mum and dad are artists but they live on an old farm and have lots of animals – as well as Tilly's dog, Bella, there are chickens and rabbits and even a goat. There are a few barns and outhouses on their land, and most of them aren't used any more. If Neon was careful, he could hide in there for a week or so without anyone ever noticing.

"You wouldn't mind living in a barn for a while until we sort something out? We'll get you a really thick sleeping bag and some blankets. And there aren't any cows or sheep in there – don't worry."

"It'll be like camping!" Neon says excitedly. "I love camping! Well, I've actually never done it, but I bet I'd love it."

It's a temporary solution, but the best one I've got.

Now we need to hope that Tilly doesn't hate me too much to say yes.

~

I know better than to turn up at Tilly's unannounced on Saturday morning. Her parents would insist that I come in, and then they'd bombard me with questions about how things in the bookshop are going, and what Joel's studying, and if Mutti has another novel coming out soon. They'd get all excited at the thought of me and Tilly being friends again, and then it would be sad and awkward when Tilly had to explain that we aren't.

Instead, I send her a message and ask if she can meet Neon and me at the bench by the loch. She always walks her dog after breakfast, so she'll be out anyway. The loch is miles long, and there are probably hundreds of benches parked along it, but Tilly will know which one I mean.

OK, she writes back. *Be there in half an hour.*

Neon and I only have to wait a few minutes before she turns up with Bella, her gorgeous cocker spaniel with the cutest floppy ears. My heart leaps when I see the dog straining on her leash, half dragging Tilly behind her.

"Hi. Hey, Bella!"

I kneel down to pet her. I hadn't realised how much I'd missed this dog. We once looked after her when Tilly and her family went to Hong Kong for a month, and, by the end of her stay, Bella would fall asleep by my feet every night.

Tilly lets me fuss over Bella for a few minutes, then takes the dog off the leash to have a wander around. She looks from me to Neon, her eyes wary. "So, what's this about?"

"We have a favour to ask," I say. "It's a really, really big one, and I don't even expect you to say yes. But right now it's our only option."

"I've decided to stay here a little longer," Neon says, smiling. "I don't want to go back to – to the place that I came from. I want to stay with Laurie instead."

"But our house is too small," I add. "And you know my mums. There's no way they would agree to having him there."

"They're coming back from London today so I need somewhere to sleep for a few nights," Neon says. "Just until I can work out what to do long-term."

"So I thought maybe…" My voice is getting squeaky with nerves. "Maybe he could camp out in one of the barns on the farm for a while? Your parents wouldn't even need to know."

Tilly's face goes through a whole rollercoaster of emotions while we're speaking: first she looks confused, then shocked, even angry, and finally her eyes narrow in suspicion.

"There's something you're not telling me," she says, crossing her arms. "Why don't you want to go back to New York? And what about your family?"

Neon says something about being happier here, feeling more like himself, but it's all too vague and wishy-washy, and Tilly obviously isn't convinced. It occurs to me that if we're asking this of Tilly, something that could get her into big trouble, she deserves to know the truth about what's going on. She might not accept it, but I should at least offer it to her.

"You're not going to believe this. I mean, you actually won't believe me." I fish around for the right words.

"But Neon… He comes from… He isn't exactly…"

"Real," Neon finishes. "Laurie made me up."

We tell her the whole story: how I invented Neon, then started to really believe him, and the realm of fictitious creations that he comes from. Tilly listens with wide eyes. She's always been so easy to read, at least to me – she's one of those people whose face always shows what they're feeling – but I'm not prepared for the next words out of her mouth.

"I *knew* you made him up!"

"You did?" I glance at Neon, baffled. "How?"

Tilly sits down on the bench with a bump. "Well, the fact that Neon never posted any videos of himself online was suspicious. He liked all the same music as you, and one time he shared a photo of a cake on a plate that's in your house, one that your mums bought in Greece." She shakes her head. "I couldn't believe it when he turned up at school. It was so obviously you running those accounts."

I don't know what to feel. On one hand, I'm embarrassed that someone was able to see through my lies so clearly. But, on the other, I'm so relieved Tilly believes me. It's also sort of nice to know that she still looks at my profiles, and even the profiles of people I'm friends with. I do the same with hers sometimes.

"Why didn't you tell Caitlin and Hannah if you knew?" I ask her.

Tilly makes a face like I've whipped a particularly stinky cheese out of my bag. "I didn't want to give them more ammunition against you. The way they talk to you is really horrible sometimes."

Neon nods. Part of me wants to defend Caitlin and Hannah, but I don't. They can be really good friends sometimes ... but not always. Not enough for me to stick up for them right now.

"So *every* fictional character lives in this realm?" Tilly asks. "From books and films and stuff too?"

When Neon says yes, her eyes flash with excitement. "Do you know the show *Doctor Who*? Have you ever seen any of the characters there?"

Neon launches into a story about seeing one of the Doctors at a barbecue a while ago. Tilly claps her hands and shrieks with delight, and she practically passes out when he says he's friends with the protagonist from *Shadows of the Sea*. She runs through all her favourite characters from her favourite media, and Neon has stories for five or six of them – he once helped two of the kids from *Heartstopper* out of a rowing boat that was about to tip over.

Tilly's eyes sparkle with joy. She loves stories. Last time I was in her room, it was covered with her fan art of her favourite characters. They're almost as real to her as I am. They definitely mean more to her than I do now.

"Why don't you want to go back there?" she asks. "That place sounds a thousand times better than the real world."

"It's hard to explain. When I was there, I always felt like I was real enough. But now I'm here..." Neon looks around: the vast loch in front of us, Bella sniffing around in the long grass, the wooden slats of the bench beneath our legs. "My life there isn't as full as I thought it was."

Tilly nods thoughtfully. "OK. My parents are going to an art exhibition in Inverness today. Come over this morning, and we'll find you somewhere to stay."

I forget that Tilly and I aren't friends any more and throw my arms round her. "Thank you so much. You're a life saver."

She stiffens at first, then awkwardly pats my back. When she pulls away from me, there's a small smile on her face.

"It's only for a few days, though, right? Mum and Dad are both pretty busy with their work right now, but I don't know how long I'll be able to host a stowaway without them noticing."

"Right, right. A few days." Neon nods. "We'll find something else after that."

Eighteen

I've been so focused on finding Neon a place to stay that I almost forget I have to work in the shop at ten o'clock. Joel could definitely manage without me, but I can't cancel this late – I don't want him to get annoyed and tell Mum and Mutti about Neon's visit, and I don't want a lecture from them about responsibilities, either. We head home and find Joel at the kitchen table, bleary-eyed with a giant cup of coffee in his hands and a book open in front of him.

"Morning," he says through a yawn. "You're up early for a Saturday."

"I couldn't sleep." I take a packet of crumpets from the bread bin and pop two in the toaster. "And Neon was already awake, so we went for a walk."

"Oh, right." Joel takes a sip of coffee and turns the page. "Are you heading home today, Neon?"

Neon takes the jam from the fridge. "I've actually decided to stick around!"

"Only for a little longer," I add quickly. "But it's OK – he's staying with Tilly this week."

"Oh, OK." Other people would check if he'd got his

mum's permission for that, but Joel's brain runs at a limited capacity in the mornings. "Are you and Tilly friends again, then? You haven't mentioned her in ages."

"No. Well, sort of? Not really." It had felt so good to talk to her again, but I don't want to get my hopes up. If she's doing us a favour, then it's for Neon, not me. "Actually, could Neon borrow some of your old clothes? He didn't bring enough for two weeks."

Joel says that's fine, and once Neon and I have finished our crumpets they head upstairs to go through Joel's wardrobe. I run upstairs to get changed into my uniform – Mum had Every Book & Cranny T-shirts made up last year after doing an online course on branding – and look out my old phone for Neon to use. The screen is cracked, and there are only a few pounds' worth of credit left on the eSIM, but it'll do for emergencies.

Worries are starting to prickle at the back of my mind. If Neon really wants to stay here, how is he going to live? He can't sleep in Tilly's barn and wear Joel's hand-me-downs forever. He'll need a home and money, food and clothes. He'll have to go to school. Maybe it's not like that in the Realm, but there's no escaping it here.

"I'll give you a lift to the farm," Joel tells me when he comes out of his room. "Then we can go straight to the shop afterwards."

While I wait downstairs, Neon comes out of the bathroom wearing one of Joel's white T-shirts with a checked shirt. His face is pale and his hands tremble as he pulls the door shut behind him.

"Are you OK?" I ask, handing him the phone. "Did you see something again?"

His face looks the way it did the day we saw the pink rabbit appear on the street outside school, and he barely seems to notice the phone in his hand. He licks his lips, searching for the words, but before he can answer Joel appears in the hallway with his bag over his shoulder.

"Are you both ready? I've got to open the shop by ten."

Neon nods and rushes out to the car. I lock up behind me, then hurry to catch up, but Neon climbs into the back seat before I can ask any more questions. Tilly's family's farm is up in the hills behind the village, five minutes from our place by car. Neon talks non-stop as Joel drives, babbling about anything his eye lands on: crows, some purple flowers by the roadside, a cloud shaped like a croissant. He's always talkative, but today I get the feeling he's trying to distract me. He saw something back at our house. Something strange and probably fictional.

Tilly is waiting for us at the end of the lane when we reach the farm. Bella is with her and starts jumping up and barking excitedly as she sees Neon. He grabs his backpack, thanks Joel for the lift and letting him stay, and jumps out to join Tilly and the dog.

When I go to give him a hug, he whispers in my ear, "There's, uh, something in your bathroom. Try not to panic when you see it, OK? We'll figure out what to do with it this afternoon."

My stomach clenches but he gives me a look that stops me from asking any more in front of the others. He turns to Tilly with a smile. "Ready to go!"

By the time we get to the shop, it's almost ten, so there's no time for me to go home and find out what Neon left back at our house. I plan to sneak out during my break but we're surprisingly busy this morning – a few of our regulars come in to get a new Ian Rankin novel that came out a few days ago, and I spend ages helping eight-year-old twin girls pick middle-grade books with their birthday vouchers.

Usually I'd be happy that business is good, but today it makes me jittery and nervous. My mind keeps coming up with ideas as to what I might find when I get home, and each one is scarier than the last. If the thing in our bathroom looks anything like the pink bunny Neon and I saw the other day, I can handle it. But what if it's something dangerous, like a dragon or a yeti? Or, even more terrifyingly – what if Mum and Mutti discover it before I do?

By the time my parents arrive at the shop, I feel sick with anxiety. They both look tired, as they always do after travelling, but they break into big smiles when they see us. They give us all tight hugs and hand out the presents they brought home for me, Joel and Gio: fancy cupcakes, books and tote bags. They both have their suitcases with them, so clearly they haven't been home yet.

"How was London?" Joel asks, sitting back down behind the counter. "Are you the toast of the literary scene?"

Mutti laughs. "Not quite but it was nice. The launch was a lot of fun. Reviews have been good, mostly."

We have all of Mutti's books in the shop, of course, and I'm always proud to show them to people. But if I'm being honest, they're not really my cup of tea. They're hefty literary novels where nothing much happens. They've won a few awards, though, and other people seem to like them a lot.

"How has everything been here?" she asks.

"Not too bad. Quiet during the week, but we had a bit of a rush hour this morning." Joel nods to me. "Laurie worked her magic in the kids' section."

"*And* I recommended to Mrs Lancaster those Loch Ness Monster colouring books that won't shift," I tell Mum. "She bought two for her grandchildren. So only about ninety-eight to go!"

Mum is behind the till, staring at something on the computer. Her mouth is a tight, straight line. Mutti looks at her with an odd expression, then busies herself straightening the hardbacks on the new fiction table. Suddenly the room is filled with a strange tension. I've known for a while that something is going on between my parents, and obviously a week in London together hasn't sorted it out. For a moment, I'm about to ask, but then I chicken out – I'm not sure I want to know the answer.

Joel breaks the awkward moment by clapping his hands together. "Hey, did Laurie tell you she sang at Friday Showcase?"

"What?" Mutti whirls round with a hardback in each hand. "You did? Laurie! That's amazing!"

My cheeks go bright red. Joel was so busy with his uni work last night that he forgot to ask about our performance, and I was too embarrassed to bring it up myself. "I didn't, actually. I was going to sing with my friend, but I got too nervous."

"Oh. Well, that's OK. You can try again another time,"

Mum says gently. "Which friend were you performing with?"

"This boy called Neon." Talking about him to my parents feels strange, but this is a small town. They're sure to bump into him eventually. "He's visiting from America. He's a really good singer, so we thought we'd try it out."

"Yeah, we've seen a *lot* of Neon this week." Joel smirks at me. I glare back at him and he holds up his hands in surrender. "Sorry about the nerves, though. You guys sounded great when you were practising."

Mum tells us to head home early – she and Mutti have some business to discuss with Gio, apparently – so Joel grabs our jackets from the back room and we head out to the car. I think about asking him if he knows what the strange atmosphere between Mum and Mutti is about, but I'm too preoccupied with whatever is currently in our bathroom. As soon as Joel pulls up on our street, I open the door and sprint towards the house.

"What's the rush?" Joel shouts after me.

"I need to pee!"

Carrie is standing at her front window but I'm in too much of a hurry to act casual this time. I quickly unlock the door, kick off my shoes and hurry upstairs to the bathroom. When I pull open the door, a scream rolls up through my body and I have to clamp both hands over my mouth to stop it from escaping. Standing in the bath, surrounded by bottles of shampoo and condition, is a *horse*. A small white horse with a silvery mane…

Wait.

It's not a horse. It's something else. And if Neon's arrival was a surprise, this is ten times more so.

Because it's a unicorn.
There is a *unicorn* in the bathroom.

Nineteen

The unicorn gazes calmly at me from the bathtub. A faint haze shimmers all round its white body, almost as if it's glowing. Its horn is the colour of mother-of-pearl, its hide is like creamy velvet bathed in moonlight, and its huge amethyst eyes sparkle in the light streaming in from the window.

It is, without a doubt, the most beautiful thing I've seen.

It's also impossible to believe I'm really seeing it. I squeeze my eyes shut, sure the mirage will have evaporated when I open them again, but the unicorn is still there. The bottles of shampoo that usually line the edge of the bath have been knocked to the ground and one has leaked a large pink puddle on the floor. I grab a towel from the radiator, kneel down and wipe it up. I need to do something normal. I need to feel the fabric against my fingers and remind myself that I'm still in the real world because this … this is *way* too much.

"Neon," I whisper. "What have you got us into?"

When I look up, still holding the damp towel, the unicorn is staring at me with those serene, shimmering eyes. On closer inspection, it's smaller than a horse, more the size of a Shetland pony, but somehow it seems to take up more space than either.

"How did you get here?" I ask, though it's obviously come from the Realm. That's the only explanation. I just don't know how, or why.

Neon said characters can only move across when people in the real world believed in them strongly enough. I went through a bit of a unicorn obsession when I was five, but even then I didn't think they were real. So, how is it here in our bathroom?

Moving very slowly with both hands held palms up, I stand and take a step towards the creature. To my surprise, the unicorn comes towards me and nuzzles its head into my open hand. Its mane is much softer and finer than horse hair, or my own. As I gently run my fingers over it, I start to feel like I'm slipping into a dream. A sense of total peace comes over me, and for a moment all I want is to stay in this bathroom forever, stroking the unicorn's mane...

I blink and shake my head. I have to deal with this before my mums get home, but I'll need help to do it. Neon and Tilly are too far away, and it would take them too long to walk here. I could call Caitlin or Hannah, but that would mean catching them up on the whole Realm situation, and I don't really trust them to keep their mouths shut.

That leaves Joel. The thought makes my knees go wobbly, but he's my only option.

Shuffling sounds behind the wall tell me that he's gone into his room. I whisper to the unicorn to stay put – it stares back at me with that same calm look – then close the bathroom door behind me and, taking a deep breath, knock on Joel's door.

"What is it, Laurie? I'm working on my essay."

"It's kind of urgent!" I push the door open a crack. "And I can see a cat video open on your screen."

"I was *about to start* working," Joel mutters. He sighs and rubs his forehead. "I don't know what's wrong with me. I can't think of a single thing to write."

"Please, Joel? I'm serious. I really need your help."

Frowning, Joel gets up and follows me out. I pause before going into the bathroom again, my fingers curled round the handle. Once I open the door, there's no going back. Joel will be in on mine and Neon's secret. Our relationship will be changed forever, whether he believes me or not.

"So…" I take a breath. "Try not to scream, OK?"

Joel's eyes widen. "Um, OK? What have you got in there?"

Instead of answering, I push the door open. When Joel sees the mythical creature standing in the bath, he does more than scream – he lets out a string of swear words and stumbles back, flapping his arms.

"Laurie! Why is there a *horse* in the bathroom?!"

"It's a unicorn," I stammer, pointing to its horn.

"A what?" Joel runs a hand through his hair. "A *what*?! Unicorns aren't real, Laurie. That's a horse. Or a pony, at least. Some sort of equine thing."

"I know they're not real. But look at it, Joel! It's obviously not a horse. It has purple eyes! It's *glowing*!"

Moving very slowly, Joel gets to his feet and approaches the unicorn. The creature gazes at him, its eyes wide and unblinking, then tilts its head towards him like it did with me. Joel leans in to inspect the horn. When his breath catches in the back of his throat, I know he's convinced.

"What's going on, Laurie?" He falls back against the wall. I've never seen his face so pale. "This is something to do with Neon, isn't it? Who is that boy?"

The only option now is the truth. I tell Joel everything I know, from the day I made Neon up to the moment I walked into the bathroom five minutes ago and found an actual unicorn in there. Joel listens to the whole story without interrupting. Even when I've finished, my usually talkative brother seems lost for words.

"Laurie... This can't be true," he says softly. "A realm where all fictional characters live? You do realise how ridiculous that sounds?"

"Trust me, I know. I almost passed out when Neon stepped off the train last Saturday. But if you don't believe me about him, at least believe me about this." I point at the unicorn's horn. "That's hardly a roll of paper and some superglue. It's real. *She's* real."

I have a feeling that the unicorn is female. Joel takes a small step towards her, then another one. He slowly puts his hand on her mane and runs a hand through the shimmering strands of hair. I suddenly remember that Joel was bitten by a horse on a school trip when he was seven and hasn't liked them since, but, as he strokes the unicorn's mane, all the tension seems to seep out of him. For a few minutes, we stand in silence, basking in the creature's glow. But then a car honks outside and I'm brought back to the real world, and the very real problem of what to do with her.

"Should we tell Mum and Mutti?" I ask.

Joel shakes his head. "No way. They've got enough on their plates without worrying about mythical creatures in the bathroom."

"What do you mean? What else are they worried about?"

"Just… Nothing, don't stress about it." Usually I would push him for an answer, but it's hard to focus with the unicorn here. Joel blinks and shakes his head, like he's trying to wake himself up. "We need to get her out of here."

"We can take her to Tilly's farm," I say. "Neon's sleeping in the barn. He can look after her."

"He's sleeping in the *barn*?" Joel throws his arms up in exasperation. "Jesus, Laurie, it's October! He'll freeze! Do Tilly's parents know he's there?"

"I'm not sure. I think so." Another lie, and one Tilly's parents wouldn't be happy about – they're not the type of people to leave a guest sleeping in a barn, especially not a teenager. I sigh. "OK, fine. No, they don't."

"Wow. Your decision-making has been really impressive lately."

"I didn't know any of this was going to happen!" I snap. "I made up a boy and suddenly he was there at the train station. It's not my fault."

The unicorn takes a step back and knocks over a bar of soap from the edge of the bath with her tail. She seems upset by the tension between us, and that's enough to make both Joel and me calm down and lower our voices.

"OK, OK. Sorry." My brother sighs and runs a hand through his hair, still completely baffled. "The most important thing is that we get her out of here before Mum and Mutti come home. Let's just pray we can do it without anyone spotting her."

Twenty

Joel brings the car round to the front door, then comes back to the bathroom to help me take the unicorn downstairs. At first we try to carry her together, but it's easier for Joel to do it himself – she weighs about as much as a packet of marshmallows. I run ahead and open the car door. Before Joel steps out, a voice makes me jump.

"Hiya, love." I turn round to see Carrie sitting on her front step. "How are things?"

"Oh, f-fine, thanks," I stammer. My eyes flit to Joel: he's frozen in the doorway, the unicorn cradled in his arms like an oversized puppy. "How are you?"

"Not so good, to be honest." Carrie sighs. "I heard this morning that the puppet theatre in Estonia that I worked for has closed down. Those were three of the best years of my life."

My heart sinks – we're going to be stuck here for half an hour if Carrie launches into one of her stories. I need to create a distraction fast.

"Oh, I'm sorry. Actually, Carrie, I was wondering if you had the recipe for that shepherd's pie you brought us the other day? It was so good, I want to try making it myself."

Her eyes light up. "Of course I do! You know me, I keep everything. Come on in. I'll find it for you."

She turns and beckons for me to follow her inside. I stare at Joel as I walk past, telepathically telling him to hurry out while he can. Still hidden in our doorway, he nods and shifts the unicorn in his arms. If we weren't in such a hurry, I'd take a photo – it's the weirdest sight I've ever seen in my life, and also one of the best.

Inside, I follow Carrie down her hallway. I've only been in her house a couple of times. She babysat Joel and me quite often when we were younger, but she always came to ours since all our toys and games were there. The place looks a lot more normal than you'd expect from someone as quirky as her, except for a few very Carrie touches – she's got a framed photo of herself shaking hands with Nelson Mandela in the hallway and a tapestry of the solar system that she made herself hanging up in her living room. She turns into her kitchen and opens a drawer beside the sink.

"It's somewhere in here…" Carrie begins riffling through hundreds of scraps of paper and newspaper clippings. There are so many that I doubt she'll be able to find what she's looking for but, after a few seconds, she pulls one out and waves it at me. "Got it!"

"Thanks so much." I carefully fold the recipe and slip it into my back pocket. "I'd better go. Joel's giving me a lift over to my friend's house. I'll let you know how the pie turns out!"

I hurry out but Carrie follows me down the hallway. "How did your performance go? I heard you and your friend practising the other day – you sounded great. I love a bit of Journey. I saw them in Osaka in 2004, while I was playing Shrek at Universal Studios."

"Oh, I actually decided not to do it this time. I get really bad stage fright, but…"

I stop abruptly as I reach the front door. To the right of the hallway is the living room, with Carrie's squashy yellow sofa and the fireplace in view. Lined up on the mantelpiece are a dozen unicorns. One is in a snow globe and one is in an open music box, but the rest are figurines in various shades of pink, white and purple.

"Do you like unicorns, Carrie?"

She follows my gaze to her collection. "Oh, I love them. My friends and family always get me one on my birthday. I know it's a bit silly but they make me happy. They're so magical, aren't they?"

I nod weakly. "Really magical." I pause, unsure of how to phrase my next question. "But you don't … think they're real, do you?"

Carrie looks confused but laughs lightly. "Well, I know I'm not going to spot one any time soon, but I'm sure they existed at one stage! There have been some skulls found in Siberia that look like they belonged to unicorns, and there's a painting of one in the Lascaux Cave in France – those are some of the oldest paintings in the world. Plus, they're Scotland's national animal, so it makes sense they would have existed at some stage."

I don't point out that the national animal of Wales is a red dragon and you don't see many of those flying around, either. This must be how the unicorn got here – because Carrie believes in them enough to have summoned one. I've always thought she was a bit eccentric, but I didn't think she was believes-in-mythical-creatures eccentric.

She tells me about how unicorn sightings have been recorded by cultures all across the world, her words picking up speed as she gets swept up in the explanation. I steal a glance through the front door. The back of Joel's head is now visible in the car window. Looks like the coast is clear.

"That's amazing," I blurt out. "Joel's waiting for me, but we should talk more about this another time."

"I'd love that, Laurie. Come round whenever you like."

Carrie says goodbye, waves to Joel and closes the door behind me. When I get back to the car, the unicorn is sitting quietly across the back seat with a blanket over her head to shield her from view. I try to pull one of the seat belts over her but she's too big, so I climb in beside her and drape an arm across her instead.

"Is she OK back there?" Joel glances at the unicorn in the rear-view mirror. "Make sure nobody sees her!"

"Don't worry, she's fine." I take a nervous look around. "But drive extra carefully."

Ten minutes later, we arrive at the farm, leave the car at the bottom of the road and lead the unicorn up the path. We crouch behind the hedges as we draw closer to the farmhouse, checking Tilly's parents aren't around, then hurry down to the barn. I throw a pebble at the door before we go in. Neon's face peeks through the gap – then falls when he sees the unicorn.

"You brought it *here*?! What if someone saw you?"

"Well, we can't keep her at ours," I snap. "What were you thinking, putting her in our bathroom?"

Tilly follows him out. She lets out a shriek, then clamps both hands over her mouth when she sees who Joel and

I have with us. "Is that…"

"A unicorn," Neon says, sighing. "I know, I know, I shouldn't have left it there like that. I'm sorry. But it was standing at the bottom of Carrie's garden. I had to get it out of sight before she noticed it."

The unicorn's glow has become brighter. She seems happier here, in the wide open space and fresh air, than she was in the bathtub or the back of our car. She stomps at the ground and trots round us in a circle, throwing back her head and shaking her shimmering mane.

Tilly looks anxiously towards the farmhouse. "Let's go inside. My parents are back. I don't want them spotting it."

The barn is already set up for Neon: there's a sleeping bag laid out on top of a pile of hay, a space heater hooked up to a portable battery, and some pumpkin-shaped fairy lights hanging from the beams. I feel a rush of nostalgia remembering all the times Tilly and I played here as kids. We tried to have a sleepover once but we got scared by the mice scurrying around and owls hooting outside and snuck back to her bedroom. Her parents had warned us that would happen, but they were nice enough not to say, 'I told you so.'

We beckon to the unicorn to follow us towards the hay, then gesture at her to sit. She lies down elegantly beside me, crossing her hooves and blowing her fringe out of her face.

"How did she get here?" Tilly asks, gawping at her.

"It's because Carrie believes in unicorns."

I fill them in on our conversation back at her house. A few hours ago, Joel would have found the idea of Carrie being a devout unicorn believer absolutely hilarious, but now he doesn't even grin.

129

"Surely this can't be a coincidence," I tell Neon. "Not after the pink rabbit that we saw."

"Um, sorry?" Joel looks from me to Neon and Tilly, who returns his blank expression with a shrug. "What pink rabbit?"

Neon and I are both too focused on the problem at hand to answer him right away. Neon sighs and rubs his face. "You're right. There's no way three of us would all turn up in the same small town unless something strange was going on."

"Well, can you take her back?" I ask Neon. "Is there, like, a portal somewhere?"

He shakes his head. "It doesn't work like that. There's not some door that magically appears for us to hop through. Before I came here, I had this odd feeling – it was like I was in two places at once, here and there, and I could choose to step fully into the real world or stay in the Realm. Then I blinked, and I was standing on the train as it arrived in Inverness."

"So how does anyone get back?" Joel asks.

"I think you can tap into that feeling again and take a step in the opposite direction. Going back shouldn't be as difficult as coming here. We're supposed to be there." Neon presses his lips together. "It's a bit more difficult with animals and other characters, though. Some of them act like humans, so they can follow instructions. You could tell them it's time to go and they would understand, even though it might be tricky to get them to actually do it."

"But what about her?" I ask. The unicorn looks up at me with her sparkling amethyst eyes, as if she knows we're talking about her.

"Maybe," Neon says, nodding. "Unicorns are smart. I'm sure she'd understand."

He shuffles on the ground so he's facing the unicorn. He gently puts both hands on her muzzle and looks deep into her eyes. The unicorn meets his gaze, and for a long moment it seems as if some silent current of communication is passing between them. But then she gives a light, tingling whinny and tosses her mane towards Neon. She knows what he's asking. But, like Neon, she doesn't want to do it.

Neon sits back on his heels and sighs. "I guess I could take her myself. I'd need to hold on to her and lead us both back. It wouldn't be hard." He bites his lip. "The thing is, I don't know if I'd ever be able to get back again."

"Surely it'd be easier now?" Tilly asks. "Loads of people believe you're real – everyone you've met at school, all the people in town."

"That's true," Neon says, "but if they know I've done it once, they might stop me from leaving again. I don't want to take that risk."

"Who are 'they'? Actually don't tell me. I don't think my brain can handle any more of this." Joel rubs his eyes and looks at each of us in turn. "You three need to sort this out. And if you want to do it before Tilly's parents find a literal *unicorn* in their barn, you'd better do it fast."

Twenty-one

Our house smells amazing when Joel and I eventually get home, which is usually a sign that Gio is in the kitchen. Mum and Mutti have him over a couple of times a month, and a few years ago he gently suggested that he take over the cooking when he comes. It turned out he's a phenomenal chef, so now my parents buy the ingredients and let him do his thing. I come in to find him standing over the stove with two steaming pans in front of him.

"Hey, Laurie." He waves a wooden spoon at me. "How does mango chicken curry and coconut rice sound?"

"Sounds amazing."

I drop my bag and give him a hug. We left the house in such a hurry that I haven't eaten since breakfast, except for some crisps and biscuits that Tilly brought to the barn earlier in the afternoon, and my stomach growls at the sight of the curry.

"Where are my mums?"

"Still in the shop. They had a few things to finish up, so they told me to head over and get started." Gio waves a wooden spoon at Joel, who has come in after me. "Where have you two been this afternoon?"

I glance at Joel. "Out to see some friends. Joel picked me up."

"Yeah, I've been studying all afternoon so I thought it would be good to get out for a bit." Joel's voice is higher than usual and he keeps scratching at the dent in the kitchen counter where Mutti dropped a cast-iron pan years ago. "Plus, I don't drive at all when I'm at uni so I'm trying to fit in a bit of practice."

One thing I've learnt about lying is that it's best not to overexplain. Joel clearly hasn't picked up on that, but fortunately Gio doesn't seem to notice anything unusual.

"Good. I'm glad you're taking a break." He tastes his sauce, then adds a bit more curry powder. "I've made a dairy-free tiramisu for dessert so I hope you two are hungry."

Joel and I set the table, and Mum and Mutti come in a few minutes later. My shoulders tense when I hear the door open, worried that the awkward atmosphere back at the shop will have followed them home, but they relax when I hear Mutti's loud, crow-like laughter.

"Hi, duckies." She unwraps the scarf from around her neck and drapes it over the back of a chair. "Good afternoon?"

I glance at Joel. "Um, yeah. Nothing special."

"Yup. Yup." Joel nods about ten times in a row. "Just a regular Saturday."

Dinner feels so normal that I almost start to wonder if I imagined our strange afternoon with the unicorn. Mutti tells us more about her events in London – the interviewer who got the hiccups and went beetroot-coloured trying to hold them in, the audience member who had "more of a comment than a question" then rambled on about Henry VIII for five whole minutes.

Gio gives us an update on his triathlon training and makes us laugh telling us about a customer who came in asking for a specific book with a scarlet cover, only to remember it was actually green after Gio had spent twenty minutes searching the shop for anything with a hint of red.

"What about you two?" Mum looks around the kitchen. "You tidied up well after all those parties, I see."

Joel forces a laugh. "Yeah, we did a pretty good job."

"It was fine," I say. "A totally normal week."

We fall into silence, both worried that we'll give something away if we speak too much. It seems so obvious to me that there's something we're keeping from them, but Mutti and Mum are distracted and don't notice. Once we've finished eating, Mum makes teas and coffees for everyone and Mutti gets a half-eaten box of chocolates down from the cupboard. I challenge Joel to a thumb war for the last strawberry one, but he smiles and tells me to have it.

"Listen, kids, we've got something to tell you." Mum has a strange, sad smile on her face. Mutti puts her hand on top of hers and squeezes it. "Mutti and I talked a lot while we were down in London, and we've made a decision."

The chocolate slips from my fingers. All the tension, the snapping, the weird looks – I know what this means. A lump bobs up in my throat and tears start to prickle at my eyes. "You're splitting up, aren't you?"

"Of course not, darling!" Mum reaches out with her other hand and takes mine in hers. I catch my breath and blink back the tears, feeling relieved but also silly. "But it is bad news – we're going to have to close the shop."

"*What?*" The word comes out as a shriek. "Mum, no!"

Mutti's face is grim. "We've just not been bringing in enough money since the tourist boats stopped coming. Honestly we're in a lot of debt, and we don't want it to get any bigger."

"That's why I was in London this week. I had a few meetings with a chain that I thought might want to take it over, but it doesn't look like it's going to work out." Mum gives a heavy sigh. "So I think it's time to say goodbye."

My eyes start to water all over again. I've known for a while that this news could be on its way, but that doesn't make it any less painful to hear. Mum opened the shop when I was five. I've grown up between those bookshelves, whiling away Saturday mornings reading in a comfy chair as my parents worked. There's not much left in this town to be proud of, but I've always been really proud that my family owns Every Book & Cranny.

"What about Gio?" I ask, suddenly feeling bad that I didn't think of him first. "What will you do?"

"Don't worry about me. Liv warned me this was likely a few weeks ago, so I already have a couple of interviews lined up." He ruffles my hair. "I'm sad it's closing, of course. But I'll still be around to cook for you once a fortnight. I need to make sure you're getting at least *one* decent meal."

"What are you going to do for work, then?" Joel asks Mum, after she and Mutti have defended their cooking skills. My brother's voice is gruff and sad. He loves the shop too.

"I'll find something to tide us over for the next few months, but long-term… I'm not sure. Maybe I'll go back to university, study something new."

"You could go to St Andrews," Mutti says, grinning. "Go partying with Joel."

Joel gives a short laugh. "Please don't."

"Don't worry, darling. My party days are over." Mum gives us both another wobbly smile. "But it'll be fine. This change could be a good thing. For all of us."

Mutti nods and puts her arm round Mum's shoulders. Their eyes are glassy and it makes mine sting harder. I know Mum's putting on a brave face for me and Joel. Owning a bookshop was always her dream, and she worked so hard to make it happen. There's no way she's happy to let it go, even if it gives her the chance to try something new.

I know I'll start crying if I sit around talking any longer, so I offer to do the dishes. Memories from the shop flicker through my mind as I scrub our plates. I had my seventh birthday party in there – Mutti ordered cupcakes decorated like my favourite books from Robbie in the bakery. Another time, Tilly and I built a fort out of paperbacks in the children's section. Mum was annoyed about it at first, but the customers didn't mind. Some of them even helped us with the roof.

I'm so lost in thought that it's a while before I notice someone outside. A person dressed in a long coat and hat stands on the pavement on the other side of our street, staring at the house on the corner where the little kid with the imaginary bunny friend lives. There's something strange about the figure. Perhaps it's a trick of the light, but I can't tell what colour their clothes are. They seem to have no real hue at all, not even the palest beige.

"Joel?" I say, turning to look at him. "Joel, can you come here?"

My brother gets up with a panicked look in his eye. Mutti watches him curiously, but she's listening to Gio talk about the book he's reading and doesn't comment. When I look back through the window, the person has disappeared. A shiver runs through me.

"What's wrong?" Joel whispers. "Is it Neon?"

I shake my head. "Nothing, sorry. False alarm."

He gives me a dubious look, but shrugs and sits down again. I shake off the unsettled feeling and tell myself I'm imagining things. Joel and I have had enough weirdness to put up with in the last twenty-four hours. We don't need any more.

Twenty-two

Sunday starts with my usual shift at Every Book & Cranny. Mutti comes with me to let Mum have a lie-in and gets me to sort out the filing cabinet in the back room before the customers start to arrive. Normally I would moan about that, but now I'm not sure how many more days I'll get to work here. I try to commit it all to memory: the slightly dusty, papery smell; the tinkle of the bell on the door when someone comes in; even the chaos of the back room, which is crammed full of stock and paperwork and old T-shirts. All week my head has been filled with Neon and the unicorn and even that silly pink rabbit. For now, I try to stay in the real world.

While I rearrange nine years of paperwork, Mutti sits at the counter on her laptop. She's already hard at work on edits for her next book, which is due out in a year. I hear a lot more sighing and muttering than typing, so it's obviously not going well.

"I don't know what's wrong with me. I can't get anything out today." She leans back in her chair and rubs her eyes. "Fancy a cup of tea?"

I sit back and realise my legs have gone stiff from

crouching down so long. "Yes, please."

Mutti makes us each a cup, then gets Mum's emergency biscuits down from the top shelf. The back room is too cramped for us both to stand in comfortably and there still aren't any customers, so we take our mugs up to the pulpit and settle into the cosy reading chairs there. The tea is exactly how I like it, nice and milky, and it actually makes me feel a little better.

"What do you think this place will be turned into once it closes down?" I ask Mutti.

"No idea, Laur." She peels off the wrapping on the biscuits. "What would you like it to be turned into? What's the town missing?"

I think for a moment. "Maybe an escape room. Or a karaoke place."

Mutti laughs and passes me the packet. "Both great ideas. You should start a petition, see if you can get the community on board."

"If I was going to start a petition, it would be to save the shop." My heart quickens. "Do you think that could work?"

"It's a bit late for that, ducky." Mutti smiles sadly. "I love that you'd be ready to do that, though."

I try to imagine the space around me with all the books gone, the cosy armchairs vanished, all my recommendations cards ripped up and thrown away. Most likely the place will sit empty for months or years before anyone rents the space for a new business, and that makes me even sadder.

"Is there anything bothering you?" Mutti looks at me as she blows on her tea. "Other than the news about the shop,

I mean. You seemed a little far away at dinner last night. Joel too."

I take a hasty gulp of my drink and try to come up with an excuse. Mutti dunks her biscuit into her tea and waits, not pushing me for an answer. Between promo for her latest book and edits for the next one, she's been really busy over the past couple of months. It's been a while since we had any alone time together. Of both of my parents, she's definitely the one more likely to believe me about Neon. I decide to test the waters.

"Mutti," I say slowly, "how *real* do you think stories are?"

She looks confused by my question. "How real? Well ... I think they have a real impact, if that's what you mean. They're mirrors for how we see ourselves." Her eyes start to shine – this is one of her favourite topics. "That's why representation is so important. Especially for queer people, people of colour, disabled people, all sorts of marginalised groups. Stories can help people feel seen and included, or show them what they can achieve."

"Definitely."

We've had this conversation before. I've talked about it with Tilly in the past too, about how much she likes finding books written by British Chinese authors or shows with Asian actors playing the main characters. And I still remember getting really excited the first time someone gave me a picture book featuring a family with two mums.

"But I also think it's important not to get too swept up in fiction," Mutti says. "Things can be more black and white in stories than they are in the real world. It's not a replacement for real life. Sometimes, when you and Joel were younger, I'd be so caught up in the plots I was creating that I'd miss things that were happening in our lives. I regretted that afterwards."

I wonder if I've done the same. After I made Neon up, I spent so much time imagining his life in New York City that sometimes I hardly noticed the world around me. At times that was what I needed, especially when things were tough with Caitlin and Hannah. But I wonder how much I missed.

Before I can think about how to broach the topic of Neon, the door opens and a customer comes in. Mutti quickly finishes her tea and hurries back down to the till. A few more people come in after that, and there's no chance to pick up our conversation where we left off.

⁓

Once my shift is over, I head home for a quick lunch, then cycle up to Tilly's to see Neon and the unicorn. There are voices coming from inside the barn when I arrive. I push open the door and find the unicorn curled up in a pile of hay with Neon and Tilly, who are both hand-feeding her carrots like she's a spoilt Roman emperor.

Neon looks up at me and grins. "Hey! We've been trying to work out what this one eats. Turns out she loves carrots, so I guess she's not totally unlike a horse."

Bella is sitting in the corner, her chin resting on her paws, obviously miffed that the attention has been pulled away from her. I kneel down to stroke her between the ears before going towards the unicorn. She turns her head to look at me and gives a soft whinny. It's the first sound

I've heard her make. It's light and musical, almost like bell chimes.

"She looks happy," I say, gently touching the unicorn's mane. The fine silvery strands glimmer in the glow of the fairy lights above us.

"Isn't she the most beautiful thing ever? Except Bella, obviously," Tilly adds, with a guilty look over at her dog. "We've been trying to come up with a name for her. Do you have any suggestions?"

I was thinking about that too, but nothing comes to mind. Tilly takes out her phone and searches for ideas – there are a surprising amount of articles dedicated to suggestions for unicorn names. We try out a few from one list: Celestia, Calypso, Luna... The unicorn doesn't react to any of them but, when she hears Tilly read out Aurora, she throws back her head and makes that light, tinkling sound again.

"I guess Aurora it is," Neon says cheerfully as Tilly laughs and pats Aurora's back. "Was everything OK at yours last night? Joel didn't tell your moms about her, did he?"

Aurora finishes one carrot and looks up expectantly. I reach for another from the bag, and she takes a big, happy bite. Bella gives a snort of disgust and slips out of the barn to go and sulk.

"No, no. You don't need to worry about that," I say. "But I do have bad news. My mums have to close down the shop."

"No!" Tilly slaps her hands to her cheeks. "I love Every Book & Cranny!"

Neon jumps to his feet. "We have to save it!" he shouts, exactly like I knew he would.

"I don't think there is any saving it," I say sadly. "Mum says they're in a lot of debt. She sounds pretty sure that this is the end of the road."

"So much stuff here has closed down," Tilly says, nodding. "And it must be so hard for bookshops to keep going when they're up against those huge online stores that can sell things much cheaper."

"Come on! There has to be something we can do." Neon starts to pace, tapping his bottom lip thoughtfully. "We need to get the word out about the place, right? Get more customers in?"

"We could bring Aurora to visit." Tilly grins and loops her arms round the unicorn's long neck to give her a hug. "Might be a bit of a tight squeeze, but that would definitely attract attention."

Neon claps his hands together. "What about an event? That would bring people to the shop!"

"They do host events sometimes – Mutti's had book launches there before, and some other local authors have too."

They've also tried to do reading groups and things, but since the pandemic only a few people have showed up. Mum's last attempt was a slam poetry evening, but so few people came that it didn't even cover the cost of keeping the shop open late.

"But they didn't have *us* to promote it! We can tell everyone at school, get them all to come. How about an open-mic night?" Neon spins round to point at me. "We could sing together! You said you wanted to try again. This could be our chance."

My stomach instantly fills with anxiety at the thought of

performing – or, worse, trying and failing to perform – in front of people for a second time. "The place is a bit small for that, isn't it?"

"We'll move some stuff around. Maybe we could borrow some chairs from school, for people who need them, and others could stand. And we could bake some cakes to sell!"

Deep down, I know that if the event was a success it would be a one-off. There's no way we'd be able to raise enough money to actually save the shop. But Neon seems so excited by his idea and so keen to help, and that's hard to say no to. He bounces on the balls of his feet, willing me to agree, and eventually I throw my hands up and laugh.

"It's worth a go, I guess."

"Awesome." Neon punches the air. "We need to do it soon. How about Friday?"

Tilly shakes her head. "Halloween is on Friday. Loads of people will be out trick-or-treating, and we don't want to clash with the school disco. Let's do Saturday instead."

We start throwing out names of people we know who might want to perform. Neon's a definite yes, of course, and I might join him if I can muster up the courage by then. Tilly's friend Jamie wants to be a stand-up comedian, which shocks me as she seems really shy.

"Um, I could have a go at performance poetry." Tilly's cheeks go bright red. "I mean, my poems are really bad, but I could give it a try."

I didn't know she wrote poetry. I'm about to say so but I hold myself back. Tilly has changed since we were best friends in primary school, and that's OK. I'm not the same person I was back then, either.

"Bet they're not," I say. "I'd really like to hear them."

"Me too!" Neon sticks one hand out. After a beat, Tilly and I place ours on top of his. "We can do this, I just know it. We're going to save Every Book & Cranny."

Twenty-three

Neon and I decide to make posters about our bookshop rescue event at lunchtime the next day. Tilly is at Dungeons and Dragons Club with Jamie and Elsie, but she said she'll come to the shop with us after school to deliver the posters before she and Neon get the bus back to the farm. When the bell rings, the two of us head to the library and sit by one of the computers. Neon looks up a free design platform and opens a blank page.

"Right." He spins round on the computer chair. "What should we write?"

I stare at the white rectangle on the screen. Nothing comes to mind. Working out what to say on the poster should be easy – I know the shop so well, and I know what we've planned to do to save it. But I can't think of any creative ways to put that into words. For some reason, my mind has gone completely blank. It was the same in Music this morning. Mr Ross asked us to come up with our own riffs on the guitar, and I couldn't even string two notes together. Half the class didn't manage, either, so I put it down to Monday-morning brain fog.

"I don't know." I shake my head to try to clear it, but the

ideas still won't come. "Write whatever you think sounds OK."

Neon types a few lines, then starts playing around with different design templates. I still can't think of a single thing to suggest, so I twirl on my chair and look round the library. The first and second years are away on a school trip, so the space is much quieter than usual – just a few fifth years working on laptops and some boys in our year playing a board game. One of the librarians, Mrs Henderson, walks by, carrying three copies of a new fantasy novel about an LGBTQ+ youth group who discover they all have superpowers.

"That's really good," I say. "My mum was sent a proof copy of it for the shop a few months ago."

Mrs Henderson gives me a sad smile. "I loved it too but I've been told I have to take it off the shelves for a while. One of the parents has complained about it, and the head wants us to leave it in storage until she can investigate whether or not it's 'suitable for young readers'."

Neon looks up from the computer. "What? Why would they do that?"

"Yeah, why?" I ask, shaking my head. "There's nothing inappropriate in it!"

Mrs Henderson doesn't say what I already know – that some people think *any* mention of queer people is inappropriate. It's stupid but it still hurts to know that someone could think that reading a simple story about people like my mums or families like ours could be damaging to kids.

"It's completely ridiculous. I'm sure the head will see that, but she wants to be cautious." Mrs Henderson pats the book at the top of the pile as if comforting it. "We had an angry email about a middle-grade book yesterday too. That was the first complaint we've been sent in years, and now here's another one. Strange."

She walks back to her desk, where she stashes the books in a drawer. I've read about book banning in other places, but I didn't think it was happening at our school. Something about it feels unusual, like it must be connected to Neon being here somehow. But, when I try to imagine why that might be, I can't come up with any ideas.

~

My mums are so excited to see Tilly, it's actually embarrassing. They bombard her with so many questions about how she, her parents, sister, grandparents and dog are doing that it takes them a few moments to even notice Neon. Remembering Joel's habit of overexplaining when he lies, I give them a very basic introduction: that Neon comes from New York and that he's visiting for a few weeks. They don't need to know more than that.

"You're the boy Laurie has been singing with!" Mutti holds her hand out to shake his. "I hope we'll get to see the two of you in concert one day."

"Well, actually…" Neon lets his backpack fall from his shoulder and pulls opens the zip. "That's sort of why we're here."

He takes out a roll of papers and unfurls it to show them one of the posters that he made at lunchtime. Mum leans in to read it, and her eyes tear up when she realises what's written on the page.

"Oh, kids." She sniffs and smiles at us. "That's a lovely idea, but I think it's too late. We'd need to take in thousands to get us out of the debt we're in."

My heart sinks. Even Neon seems to deflate as he rolls the poster back up. But Mutti puts a hand on Mum's shoulder and reaches for it.

"Maybe we should do it anyway, Liv." She spreads the piece of paper out on top of some hardbacks. "It would be a nice way to say goodbye to the place. And I want to hear these two sing!"

"Me too. I think it's a great idea." Gio leans over Mutti's shoulder to read the text. "Do you have performers ready, though? Saturday is only a few days away."

We fill them in on the line-up. Caitlin and Hannah were really excited when we asked them to perform – they're going to do a dance routine that they've been practising at their musical-theatre class. Tilly's friend Jamie took a bit of convincing, but she eventually said she'd try out her stand-up material. Mr Ross and his band are going to come, Mikey the cello prodigy is in, and then there's Tilly, Neon and me. Allowing for setting up and a bit of talk in between each act, that's probably enough to fill forty-five minutes to an hour.

"And we can leave the other slots free in case anyone else turns up," Tilly says. "We want it to be a community thing, open to everybody."

"You three have thought of everything, haven't you?" Mum looks round the shop. She lets out a long sigh, and Mutti reaches for her hand. "You're right. It'll be fun, and the shop needs a good send-off. Let's do it."

We put a poster in each window and another on the noticeboard beside the counter. After that, we stop by the supermarket, Bohemian Catsody and a few other shops and businesses along the high street to ask if we can pin some up in there too. Everyone we speak to seems genuinely sad when they hear that the shop is in trouble, and they all promise to come along if they can – Robbie from the bakery even says he'll donate a load of cupcakes and doughnuts.

Despite what Mum said about being in debt, our efforts plant a tiny seed of hope in me. Maybe we *could* actually save the place. Maybe that's the reason for Neon being here. Not to help me but to save Every Book & Cranny.

We stick a few more posters up on lamp posts and at the bus stop, then Tilly and Neon go back to the farm to check on Aurora. My mums are still at the shop, but I've got Maths homework for tomorrow so I head home.

As I turn the corner on to our street, a strange feeling comes over me. My mind goes blank like it did at school earlier today, but much worse. It's like a fog has seeped into my head, shrouding all my thoughts and ideas in a thick greyish mist. I carry on towards home, blinking rapidly to try to clear the haze, then stumble to a halt a few doors down from ours.

Standing outside our gate are two figures. One is the colourless person that I saw staring at the house on the corner on Saturday night. The other is a woman dressed in similarly nondescript clothes, with a wave of mousy-grey hair falling down her back. Their backs are turned to me and their heads are tilted back at identical angles, looking up at the windows of our house.

I take a slow step backwards, about to run, and accidentally crush an old can with my foot. Moving slowly, the pair turn to face me. All the blood drains from my face. I stumble backwards and grab the neighbour's hedge for balance, my heart pounding. I can't see their faces. No – these people don't *have* faces. Where their eyes, noses and mouths should be are nothing but blurry smudges, like the image has been rubbed out.

"Who are you?" I whisper, though maybe the question should be *what*.

Neither figure replies. They seem to be staring at me from those pale, featureless ovals, though I'm not sure if they can even see without eyes. The one that I thought was a man turns to face our house, then slowly tilts his head up to look at my window.

They're here for Neon.

A car turns the corner and its headlights sweep across the street. The figures draw back into the shadows. For a moment, I'm blinded by the lights. I shut my eyes and, when I open them again, the figures have gone. I rush into our house and double-lock the door behind me. The thick fog in my head lifts, but the fear keeps pounding through my veins long after.

Twenty-four

I send Neon a message as soon as I get in, but it's still marked unread the next morning – the signal is always patchy up at the farm. I rush to school to warn him that someone is looking for him, not even bothering to eat breakfast first. When I arrive, he's in the courtyard with Tilly, Jamie and Elsie, all huddled together and watching something on a phone.

The sight stirs up a mix of feelings. There's a bit of jealousy – Neon lived inside my head for so long, a friend just for me, and it's strange to see him hanging out with Tilly and the others on his own. But there's also happiness that Tilly and I are on speaking terms again, and nerves about how Jamie and Elsie will react if I go and join them. Tilly must have talked to them about me in the past, and I'm sure not all of it was good.

Still, that was a long time ago, and things are different now. *I'm* different now. So I take a deep breath, squash down the feelings and put on what I hope is a normal smile as I walk through the school gates.

"Laurie!" Neon throws his arms round me in a hug, and it instantly soothes my nerves. "We're watching the lion video. Did you see it?"

Jamie passes me the phone. The screen shows a blurred image of a playground, a faded slide and a set of swings. It's twilight in the shot, but I recognise the place as the park down the road. When I press play, someone off-camera lets out a muffled scream. A second later, a lion – huge, male, with an enormous fiery mane – stalks into the shot. My jaw drops.

"Whoa!" I lean in closer for a better look. The lion walks round the play park in leisurely loops, sniffing at the ground and apparently ignoring the person filming. "Where did you find this?"

"Russell sent it to me," Jamie says. "He got it from someone in fifth year. It's obviously AI, but it's really convincing, isn't it?"

Tilly, Neon and I exchange a look. We all know it's not AI, but I understand why Jamie thinks so. The lion looks too perfect: its amber eyes are bright even in the dim light, and its mane is flame-coloured rather than the ginger or sandy tones of the real animal. It saunters dangerously close to the person filming, who seems to fall over, because the camera angle swings past the trees and up to the darkening sky. By the time they get up and find the shot again, the animal has disappeared.

"Super convincing," Tilly says, nodding.

Neon puts his hand on my arm. "Off-topic, but we really need to decide what to sing for the open-mic night. We've only got a few more days to practise."

"Ugh, don't remind me." I hand the phone back to Jamie and give her a nervous smile. There's a TARDIS pin on the collar of her jacket, the same one Tilly has on her bag. "I heard you're going to do stand-up! That's amazing."

"Well, I'm going to try." She laughs and slides her phone into her pocket. "I'm so sorry about the shop, though. That sucks."

"I really hope your mums can work something out," Elsie tells me, pushing her dark hair behind her ears. "Every Book & Cranny is the best bookshop for miles."

"It really is. I told Jamie and Elsie that you recommended *Shadows of the Sea*," Tilly says, smiling at me. "Good taste."

I'm not sure what to say. I always assumed that Jamie and Elsie hated me, but they're being so nice. Maybe it's because of Neon – they like him, so they're putting up with me because I'm his friend. Or maybe they're just kind people. I guess that's why Tilly likes them so much.

The bell rings and we say goodbye and head to our separate registration classes. Once Tilly and the others have turned the corner, I tell Neon about the faceless figures lingering outside my house. As I talk, the colour drains from his cheeks. There's an expression I've never seen on him before: fear.

"Oh, man." He runs his hands over his face. "I knew they'd be furious, but I honestly didn't think they'd come all the way here to find me."

I lower my voice as a gaggle of first-year girls pushes past us. "But who are those people?"

"They're not people. They're Blanks," he says dully. "They patrol the border between the Realm and the real world. They're what stops us from leaving. Most of the time anyway. There are some cases where we slip through, like I did. Maybe they'd have let it slide if it was only me, but they can't let a unicorn, a pink rabbit and a lion wander around too."

I pause at the door to our registration classroom. Hannah waves at us from her desk in the corner. I raise my hand but can't bring myself to smile back.

"So they're here to take you away?" My stomach flips in time with the words.

Neon keeps his gaze fixed on the ground, his eyes shiny. "Probably. Either that or they'll want to erase me altogether."

"What? They can't do that!" I shake my head in horror. "Couldn't I just make you up again?"

"Maybe," he says, shrugging. "Or they could wipe me from your memory too. From everyone's. They've got the power to do that. They're the opposite of imagination, creativity, curiosity. They're the absence of it. That's why we call them Blanks – because they're nothing."

Something clicks into place: the trouble I had designing our open-mic night posters, Mutti's writer's block, the way nobody could come up with the riffs Mr Ross asked us to create in Music yesterday… It's because of these things, these Blanks. They're draining the creativity and imagination out of everyone they come across.

The idea sends shivers all over my skin. But the idea of Neon being erased forever – that's beyond horrible. The future with him here is so much more complicated than he realises, but, now that it's a real option, I don't want to let go of it. He's my best friend. I can't lose another one of those.

"We should find another place for you to sleep," I whisper. "This is a small town. It won't take them long to work out you're staying at Tilly's."

Neon nods and follows me into the classroom. "You're right. Hopefully the lion will be enough to keep them off our backs for a while, but they'll come after me soon. Aurora too."

While Miss Fraser takes attendance and reads out a few updates from the headteacher's daily bulletin, I rack my brain for places that Neon could stay without getting caught. I've already ruled out most of the people I know. He could sleep in the back room of the bookshop, but it would be uncomfortable and almost impossible to get him in and out without my mums or Gio noticing. I could see if Joel or Tilly have any money that we could put together to pay for a room in one of the local B&Bs, but that would only be a temporary solution.

Neon is unusually quiet as we walk towards our first class. Some of the others notice too – Hari swings an arm round Neon's neck and gives him an energetic head rub, asking him what's up. While they wander ahead, Caitlin and Hannah catch up with me.

"Is everything OK with Neon?" Hannah asks. "He seems pretty down this morning."

Caitlin slides her arm through mine. "Did you guys have a fight? We've hardly seen you the past few days – we're so behind."

"No, nothing like that. He's…" I grapple for an excuse but I can't find one. It's like the part of my brain that comes up with ideas is on pause. "He's having a bad day."

"You know what would probably make him feel better? Kissing *you*." Caitlin grins and jostles my arm. "Come on. Tell me you've done it already."

This again. I almost sigh but I don't want to deal with

the attitude Caitlin would give me. "Not yet. Still waiting for the right moment."

"Laurie!" Caitlin drops my arm so she can throw her hands into the air. "Oh my God, you're hopeless."

"Don't say that!" Hannah ignores the dirty look Caitlin shoots her way and gives me an encouraging smile. "It's totally fine to take things slow, Laurie."

I nod, grateful to Hannah for sticking up for me, but a familiar feeling creeps in all the same. Maybe it *is* strange that I haven't kissed anyone yet. Neon and I have had more important things to worry about lately, and we haven't had much time alone, either. But maybe it's weird that I'm not thinking about it more. Maybe that's not normal.

My worries fade into the background when I see Neon waiting for me outside our History classroom. He looks so sad and anxious, so unlike his usual sunshine self. Keeping him away from the Blanks has to be our main priority. I can worry about kissing him, or not kissing him, once we've found a new place for him to stay.

That's when an idea finally comes to me. We've clearly reached the point where we need an adult's help – a real adult, not Joel this time. But it has to be the sort of adult who will take us seriously. The sort of person who is likely to listen to what we need, and not go running to my mums.

And that's probably the sort of person who believes in unicorns.

Twenty-five

"Gosh, I'm unfit." Carrie pants and wipes her forehead as we trudge up the steep path to the barn. "And to think I once ran a whole ultramarathon dressed as a hot dog."

Tilly promises her it's not much further. After school, she, Neon and I went straight to Carrie's and told her we had something important to show her. A lot of adults would insist on more information before driving us all the way up here, but Carrie seemed quite excited by the idea of a surprise. The sun is setting now, the sky turning a deep, dusky purple streaked with orange, and I can still see a glint of curiosity in her eyes as we reach the barn.

"Try not to scream," Tilly whispers, sliding the door open. "We don't want to scare her."

All I see is some flattened straw on the barn floor. My heart skips a beat, thinking that perhaps the Blanks have caught Aurora already – but then something shuffles in the corner and a shiny, glowing horn appears behind another pile of hay. Tilly goes towards the unicorn, talking softly and soothingly, and after a moment Aurora makes a dainty leap over the hay and lands in front of us.

"Carrie," I say, smiling, "this is Aurora."

For the first time since I've known her, Carrie is speechless. She stands frozen, her mouth a deep purple circle, as the unicorn trots round the barn. Aurora nuzzles her face against Tilly's first, then goes to Neon and presses her muzzle into his hand in greeting. She lets me stroke her mane to say hello, then turns her glittering amethyst gaze to Carrie. When Aurora bends her head towards her in a slight bow, Carrie's eyes brim with tears.

"I knew it," she whispers. "I *knew* it."

There are so many emotions in those few words: excitement and wonder, but some pain and vindication too. Suddenly I realise how unusual it is for Carrie to be the way she is. Most adults would feel silly having lots of unicorn ornaments on display in their house, and most would have long lost the imagination they need to actually believe in them. She must have come across loads of people who made fun of her for it, but she's stayed her eccentric self. I like that.

Aurora trots over to her sleeping spot and settles down in the hay, her tail swishing happily behind her. Tilly takes out a large bunch of carrots from her schoolbag and picks one to feed her. I take Carrie's arm and lead her over to join them.

"Where did you – how did you – when?" Carrie splutters, still shaking her head in astonishment. "Laurie, *what* is going on?"

Neon and I tell her the whole story. While we talk, Tilly gives Carrie a carrot to feed Aurora. Aurora eats it in small, neat bites and then tilts her head towards Carrie for her to stroke her mane. Carrie runs her fingers through the silky strands, and the tears in her eyes finally fall.

I don't know if she's going to be able to help us, but either way I'm glad we could give her this moment.

"Do you believe us?" I ask.

"Of course I believe you. This one is proof enough." Carrie laughs lightly and presses her hand gently against Aurora's face. "And you know, now you mention it, I *have* been feeling a bit funny lately. I did a full-moon flash-fiction workshop online yesterday and couldn't come up with a single idea. That's not like me."

Neon lets out a long sigh. "I don't know what to do. I don't want the Blanks to stick around and eat up everyone's imagination, but I don't want them to erase me or send me away, either."

"Well, first we need to get you two out of this barn," Carrie says, looking at the bare wooden walls. "If these Blank characters turn up here, you'll have no one around to help you."

She presses her lips tight together, thinking. I sit back in the hay and pick up a carrot to feed to Aurora. For the first time since Neon arrived, a weight has been lifted from my shoulders. It feels good to finally let an adult take charge.

Suddenly Carrie claps her hands so loudly it makes us all jump, Aurora included.

"I've got it. Come with me."

After a few more carrots, we lead Aurora from the barn. Tilly runs home so her parents don't start to worry, and also to keep them distracted while Neon and I take the unicorn down the path to Carrie's car. We climb into the back of the bright yellow Beetle with Aurora splayed across our laps like an oversized cat. Carrie does a U-turn on the narrow country road and drives in the opposite direction from our town. Neon asks where she's taking us, but all she says is that we're going to a friend's house.

After ten minutes, Carrie turns off the main road and down a narrow country lane. Beautiful old oak trees line the path, their branches stretching together to create a tunnel leading to a large metal gate. She stops the car and presses a number into a panel on the old stone wall. The gates slide open, and after a moment the biggest house I've ever seen comes into sight: three storeys of cream walls, countless windows and at least four turrets, all lit by the soft glow of old-fashioned lamp posts.

"Whoa!" Neon presses his face against the car window. "Who lives here?"

"This is my friend Tamara's place," Carrie says casually. "The one who asked me to look after their bonsai collection."

I've always taken Carrie's stories with a pinch of salt – sometimes an entire spoonful of salt – but it seems the one about the film director friend shooting a movie in Thailand was true. She parks the car, gets out and punches a number into a second keypad by the towering front door. Neon and I help Aurora out and then follow Carrie into an enormous hallway with a domed ceiling. The wooden floor is so shiny that Neon and I instinctively pull off our shoes so we don't trail dirt through the house.

"What do you think?" Carrie asks, grinning. "Bit comfier than a barn, eh?"

Neon gapes at a row of glittering awards lined up on a table by the door. "We can really stay here? Your friend won't mind?"

"Not at all. They always say they're happy for me to use the place." Carrie pauses. "We should probably keep Aurora away from the bonsai, though. I don't know if she'd eat them, but best not to find out."

She takes Aurora to the back garden to sleep in the dog kennel, which turns out to be a cabin-style building that could easily fit me and Neon, let alone one small unicorn. While Carrie gets her settled in, Neon and I go upstairs to pick a guest bedroom for him to use. Each one has a different theme, almost like a hotel. One is nautical, all stripes and anchors and navy blue. Another looks like a jungle, filled with so many plants you can barely see the bed, and one is painted like space, with beautiful glass planets hanging from the ceiling.

The last one has been inspired by the eighties. The walls are bright pink and the carpet is turquoise, and the bedsheets are covered in colourful geometric shapes and squiggly lines. There's a vintage record player in one corner, fancy electric guitars on a special stand by the window, and signed album covers by artists like Prince and Kate Bush hanging on every wall. When I switch on the lights, a neon sign spelling out *Good vibes only* flickers on above the bed. It's colourful and musical and perfectly Neon.

"This is it." He beams and throws his bag on to the bed. "This place was made for me."

I sit down at the foot of the bed. Neon stretches out beside me, his hands clasped behind his head, and closes his eyes. He lets out a long sigh of relief, sending all the stress of the past couple of days into the air. The light from the sign washes across his face, painting his eyelids and cheekbones in bright pink.

"Oh, man. It's going to feel so good to sleep in an actual bed. Not that I didn't appreciate the sofa bed or the sleeping bag," he adds, grinning.

I don't answer. He looks so peaceful in the pink light, so pretty. If Caitlin was here, she'd tell me to kiss him now. She'd practically *force* me to kiss him. My hand edges across the duvet until my fingertips are millimetres from Neon's. I could hold his hand. I could take this one tiny step forward – but then his eyes open, and the opportunity is gone.

"Should we see if this director's got any fancy food in the cupboards?" He sits up and swings his legs over the side of the bed. "I'm starving."

"Um, sure." My cheeks are hot with embarrassment, but Neon doesn't seem to notice. "Me too."

Downstairs, we find Carrie putting on her coat. She says she'll drive me home and pop into her house for some food, clothes and other things she needs, but will come back right away to make Neon dinner and spend the night here. Neon tells her he'll be fine on his own, but she shakes her head firmly.

"You're a kid. I don't want you here alone if those Blank things track you down." She picks up her car keys from the worktop. "Plus, that way I can drive you to school in the morning and bring you back in the afternoon."

Neon throws his arms round her and mumbles thank you into her shoulder. Carrie looks taken aback for a moment, but then she smiles and squeezes him tight. I made Neon more independent than I was, gave him more freedom than my mums would ever let me have. But he's real now, and, like Carrie says, he's still a kid. He needs someone to look after him too.

Twenty-six

The dinner table is oddly quiet that night. Mum makes massaman curry, which is one of our family favourites, but the conversation never really gets going. Everyone seems to be lost in their own world, including me. Once the dishes are done, I fetch my school tablet to do my Geography homework and Mutti and Joel whip out their computers. They sit on either side of me at the kitchen table, frowning at their screens, occasionally typing something and then deleting it. After twenty minutes, Mutti lets out a groan of frustration.

"I don't know what's happened to me." She drops her face into her hands. "I haven't finished a single paragraph since I came back from London. It's like I've forgotten how to write."

A guilty feeling niggles at me. It's not my fault that the Blanks are here, or Neon's, but our decision to keep him hidden is the reason they're hanging around. As long as they're in town, Mutti won't be able to finish the next draft of her book. Her deadline is the end of November, so she only has a month to go.

"Maybe you need more of a break," I say, forcing a smile.

"You've had a lot going on, between the London trip and everything happening with the bookshop."

"Laurie's right. You'll be fine if you let it rest for a couple of days." Mum rubs Mutti's shoulder. "How about we all play a game after Laurie's done with her homework? Something to take your mind off it."

Joel closes his laptop. "I'm in. I'm not getting anywhere with this essay, either."

Mum heads to the cupboard upstairs where we keep the board games, and Mutti goes to get the biscuits. They both come back with a few options, and we eventually decide on some fancy caramel shortbread and a numbers game, a simple one that doesn't require much brainpower. As I count out the plastic tiles for each of us, I realise something: Joel was supposed to go back to St Andrews last Sunday, after Mum and Mutti came home from London. I've been so focused on everything going on with Neon, I haven't thought to ask why he's still here.

"Youngest starts," Mutti tells me. As I'm working out the combinations I can make with my selection of numbers, she dunks a biscuit into her tea and takes a bite. "So, are you ready for the open-mic night?"

A jolt of nerves hits me at the mention of our performance. I pick out a row of consecutive numbers and move them to the centre of the table. "I think so. We've got a good line-up, and hopefully a few others will join."

Mum is to my left, so she sets out her numbers next. "What about you, Joel?" she asks. "You fancy signing up?"

Joel snorts and teases a biscuit from the packet. "What would I do? I don't have any talents."

"Yes, you do," I say, prodding him in the side. "You can act."

"Thanks, Laur, but I don't think anyone would appreciate me standing up and reciting a Shakespearean monologue." He grins and slides his tiles across the table. "But I'll be there to give moral support or be on the till, or both."

"Where did Neon come from anyway?" Mutti asks me. "He seemed to pop out of nowhere, but the two of you are such good friends already."

She glances up from her numbers, her eyes slightly narrowed. I almost wonder if she suspects something, but after a moment she looks back down at her tiles and sets three sevens in the middle of the table.

"I guess we clicked pretty fast. One of those things," I say, keeping my eyes fixed on my numbers. "And, before either of you say it, *no*, he's not my boyfriend."

Mutti smiles. "I wasn't making any assumptions. You know it would be OK if he was, though, right? We'd be totally supportive if you wanted to date a boy. Love is love!"

Joel and I both roll our eyes. Our parents never get tired of that joke.

"Thanks, Mutti," I say, laughing. "Good to know."

We play three rounds of the game. Mum wins the first, Joel the second, and I take the third before Mutti pretends to be a sore loser and flounces off to the kitchen to make more tea. While she's gone, Mum gets up to take the laundry out of the washing machine, leaving me and Joel alone. He checks they're both out of earshot, then leans towards me.

"What's going on with Neon and Aurora? Are they OK?"

Keeping my voice to a whisper, I tell him about Carrie

taking them to her friend's place. Joel seems relieved that Neon is no longer sleeping in a barn, and his jaw drops when I describe the house – it turns out Tamara Mackenzie is very, *very* famous, at least to film buffs like Joel.

"Are you all right?" I ask. "Weren't you supposed to go back to uni last weekend?"

He blinks. "Uh, yeah, I was. I've decided to stay another week or two. I'm missing a few tutorials, but most of the stuff is online anyway. I'll catch up."

"Oh. OK."

Joel was different before he moved to St Andrews. He'd play tricks on me all the time – he was always jumping out of cupboards or from behind the curtains to scare me, and one time he mixed half a bottle of extra-spicy hot sauce in with the ketchup and almost blew my head off. He could be annoying, but he laughed more than he does now. He made me laugh a lot too. He'd find really bad, low-budget movies from the eighties and nineties for us to watch together, and we'd spend the whole hour and a half laughing at the plot holes and cheesy dialogue. We used to have entire conversations in film quotes. It was like a secret language, both of us cracking up while Mum and Mutti looked on, smiling but baffled.

That changed when he went away to university. Joel still comes home a lot, but he spends more time alone in his room these days. He'll still joke around or watch films with me, but sometimes he's distant and quiet in a way he never was before. I thought he was stressed about all the work he had to do, but maybe there's something else bothering him.

Before I can ask him about it, Mutti comes back into the room with four cups balanced in her hands.

"Another round?" she asks, setting them down on the table. "I want at least one small success tonight, and it's clearly not going to be with my edits."

I smile and agree to another game, but the worries in my stomach multiply. If Neon and I don't find a way to get rid of the Blanks soon, Mutti might never write another book again.

Twenty-seven

There's a vampire outside the post office. She stands reading the notices about dog walkers and piano lessons in the window, her black hair slicked back and a red velvet cape sweeping past her ankles. When a couple of boys in the year above mine walk past, sniggering about how Halloween isn't until Friday, she hisses and bares her fangs at them. One of the boys jumps back and knocks into the post box.

"Whoa!" After a beat, the fear leaves his face and he lets out a high-pitched laugh. "Sick costume."

The vampire isn't the only strange character hanging around. Walking to school, I spot a small child so pale they can only be a ghost. There are other people I think might also have come from the Realm, people who look like anyone else, but who wander the streets staring at things like Neon would when he first arrived here. One man outside the Co-op picks up a chihuahua and examines it like a piece of fruit, which does not please its owner.

Everyone else has noticed too. At school my whole class is talking about the oddly dressed strangers they've seen around town. Luckily everyone seems to assume they're wearing costumes for an early Halloween event. Maybe the presence of the Blanks has sucked away their ability to imagine anything other than the most obvious explanation.

"We're lucky you turned up in October," I tell Neon. "This would be a lot harder to explain in July."

It's lunchtime, and Tilly, Neon and I have come to the park along the road from school. It's freezing, but we're on the lookout for any other characters that might turn up. Jamie and Elsie sat with us for a while, but eventually they got bored and cold and went back to the nice warm library.

"Speaking of Halloween," Tilly says, rubbing her hands together to heat them up, "have you two found costumes for the disco yet?"

Tilly and her friends don't usually come to school discos, but they make an exception for Halloween because they all love cosplay. This year, they're each going as a different Doctor from *Doctor Who*. They've had their costumes ready for ages. Caitlin and Hannah ordered their devil and angel outfits weeks ago too.

"I'm going to wrap a load of toilet paper round myself and go as a mummy," Neon says. "And I found a bird mask in the Art cupboard, so I'll wear that too. A mummy-crow hybrid."

"I can't believe I left it so late," I say, a wispy white sigh leaving my mouth. "I love Halloween."

Last year, I went as zombie Willy Wonka. Mum found this perfect purple coat in a charity shop, and Mutti spent ages doing my make-up to make me look like a member of the undead. The effect was actually really creepy – I'd freak out if that character ever stumbled out of the Realm.

"How about I come over to yours after school?" Tilly shifts her hands under her legs. She's always had trouble keeping them warm in winter – sometimes her fingers turn completely white. "I can help you find something."

"Oh, OK. That would be great."

Her offer takes me by surprise. We've been spending lots of time together lately, but only with Neon around. I ask him if he wants to come along, but he shakes his head.

"No, thanks. Carrie's coming to pick me up, so I'll go back to the director's house to hang out with Aurora and—" Flinching, he breaks off and points to the other end of the park. "Look! There's one over there."

Between a cluster of trees, the vampire I saw outside the post office this morning appears. Her hair is dishevelled, the edge of her cape is now caked with mud, and there's a worrying red smudge around her mouth that I hope is jam.

Neon stands up – whether to greet her or to run, I'm not sure. Before I can ask, my mind fills with a thick, familiar fog. A cold feeling floods my chest, and the world around me seems to lose some of its colour.

Tilly puts her hands to her head. "What's going on?" she whispers. "I feel really weird."

Before I can answer, a colourless figure in a long coat steps on to the path behind the vampire. Its hood falls back, revealing a blurry white oval where a face should be. Tilly lets out a strangled scream; Neon mutters a swear word and scrambles backwards. The Blank moves slowly and uncertainly towards the vampire, its arms stretched out like it's searching for its target in the dark.

The vampire spins round. She gives a loud, sharp hiss; her arms fly out to the sides, batlike in her cape. But then, before she can attack or escape, the tension seeps out of her. The Blank reaches out a hand and runs two long pale fingers down the vampire's face. The image of her body breaks into tiny pieces and blows away like dust, spinning in three loops of red and black before disappearing into nothing.

Out of the fog in my head, one thought emerges.

"Run…" I tell Neon. "*Run!*"

I don't wait to see what the Blank does next. I grab Neon's sleeve and we race out of the park, through the streets and back to school. They're getting closer, and we won't be able to run forever.

I feel jittery for the rest of the afternoon. That's mostly because of our close call with the Blank and the fear one will burst into our classroom and make Neon disappear, but the thought of Tilly coming to my house is making me nervous too. We arrange to meet at the school gates after our last class, and when she doesn't turn up immediately I start to worry that she's forgotten or changed her mind. She comes running round the corner a moment later, still pulling on her coat.

"Sorry! I had some library loans due." She shrugs her right arm into the sleeve and tugs up the zip. "Mrs Henderson told me they had complaints about *six* more books today. Isn't that crazy?"

"I wonder if that's because of the Blanks," I say. "If they're sucking the imagination out of people around here, I bet their empathy is going too."

"You're probably right." Tilly shudders, and I know we're both picturing the faceless figure in the park earlier. "Did Carrie come to pick Neon up?"

I nod. "He'll be safe at the director's house – it's miles away."

It's the first time that Tilly and I have been alone since our argument in the girls' toilets last week. That feels like a lifetime ago now. I'm worried it'll be awkward, but we exchange theories about the Blanks as we walk down the road to my house, and soon all the nerves have gone. It almost feels like old times, the days when our houses were like second homes to each other – we had so many sleepovers that we both kept extra pyjamas and toothbrushes there.

Mum's at work when we get in, but Mutti is in her home office, writing. When she hears us talking, she comes through to greet Tilly. She doesn't bombard her with questions like she did last time, but instead lists every single snack in the house – she even offers to make us pancakes. Her obvious delight that we're friends again is a bit cringe, so I tell her it's fine and grab some crisps to take up to my room.

"Sorry about that," I say, once we're safely inside. "They think you're their long-lost second daughter."

"It's OK." Tilly sits down on my bed, her eyes scanning my room for changes since she was last here. "Mine are the same. When I mentioned we were talking again, they actually gave me a round of applause."

I open my wardrobe and start pulling out things that I might be able to use for a costume. There's not much – my favourite colour is turquoise and most of my clothes are quite bright, nothing very suitable for Halloween. Tilly can't think of anything, either, so she takes out her phone and searches for ideas.

"How about that?" she says, pointing to a horrible orange jumper that someone gave me last Christmas. "You could use some black fabric to add eyes and a mouth and be a pumpkin."

"Wouldn't I look like a giant toddler?"

"Probably, but I think you could pull it off."

I laugh and toss it to her. "We'll put it in the maybe pile."

"Fair enough." Tilly lays the jumper out on the bed. She's quiet for a long moment, her lips twitching in a way that means she's weighing out exactly what she wants to say next. "I know our parents are being embarrassing about it, but … it actually has been nice hanging out together again."

My cheeks flush pink with happiness. I pull a black-and-white polka-dot T-shirt off its hanger and pass it to her. "Yeah. It has."

"It feels sort of silly that we stopped now. I was trying to work out exactly why it happened." She catches the T-shirt and adds it to the maybes. "I think I really wanted to be someone new after we started high school. I wanted a fresh start. And I felt like that meant separating myself from the person I'd been in primary school."

"That makes sense," I say, nodding.

"Did you feel like that too?"

"Not really. I was just amazed Caitlin and Hannah wanted to hang out with me. They were both really pretty and loads of boys liked them, and I was so surprised they wanted to be my friends that I felt like I couldn't say no."

I pause. "Sometimes I wonder if Caitlin only wanted someone to pick on, though."

"No, I think she actually does like you. She's just the sort of person who has to be Queen Bee." Tilly wrinkles up her nose. "I'm sorry. I feel like it's my fault you got stuck with them."

"You don't have to be sorry. Sometimes people grow apart. It's OK."

"Yeah, but they can come back together too." Tilly throws back her head and laughs. "Sorry, that sounds so cheesy."

I grin. "I don't mind cheese."

"Yeah, but that was, like, *Stilton*-level cheese."

Having her here, I finally realise how wrong my friendship with Caitlin and Hannah was. Friends shouldn't gang up on you. They shouldn't make you feel bad about yourself. You shouldn't have to hide so many parts of yourself for their approval. Maybe I invented Neon to get Caitlin and Hannah off my back, but I kept up the lie because I wanted a real friend again. A friend like Tilly.

"You must have thought it was pretty pathetic, me making up an online friend," I say, once we've agreed that her comment was, at most, a solid Wensleydale.

"It's not pathetic. Well, lying to people usually isn't a great idea. But is it really that different from getting lost in other types of stories, like books or TV shows?" Tilly shrugs. "Some of the characters I love have really changed my life. Elsie's dad is always going on at her to stop writing fanfic and get some proper hobbies, but I'm glad my parents aren't like that."

"Same," I say, though I don't know how my mums

would feel if they knew how deep I'd fallen into my story about Neon. They both love books but, like Mutti said on Sunday, fiction isn't a replacement for the real world. They wouldn't want me to let a story take over my life.

But for a little while it did. Maybe, if I hadn't been so wrapped up in my story about Neon, I would have moved on from Caitlin and Hannah sooner. I might have tried to make amends with Tilly or found another group to be part of.

"You know," Tilly says, "if Neon does have to leave, you could maybe hang out with me and Elsie and Jamie if you like? I hope he can stay, obviously. But I thought I'd say, you know. Just in case."

I try not to smile too widely, but I don't really succeed. "Thanks. You don't think they'd mind?"

"Nah, I'm sure they wouldn't. They *will* make you watch every single episode of *Doctor Who*, though."

I laugh. "I can deal with that. I actually watched a few a while back. They were good."

"You did? Which ones?!"

Tilly makes me list off every episode, then rambles on for ages about her favourites. I don't think I'll ever be a *Doctor Who* superfan like she is, but I always liked hearing her talk about the things she loves: the way her hands dart from side to side, and how her voice gets slightly squeaky when she's really excited. For the first time in almost two years, part of my life feels like it's edging back towards normal.

Twenty-eight

"Oh, Saint Billie Joe Armstrong." Neon presses his hands together and holds them up to the poster of Green Day that Mr Ross keeps pinned above his desk. "Grant us some inspiration."

It's Thursday lunchtime and we're holding a rehearsal for the open-mic night in one of the music classrooms. It's not turning out the way we'd hoped. Jamie tried out her stand-up routine, but she kept going blank and forgetting the punchlines. Tilly's poems were really good but her voice was weirdly flat, like she was reading out a shopping list. Caitlin and Hannah were similar – all the steps of their routine were in place, but the performance wouldn't pop. It has to be because of the Blanks. They're snuffing out everyone's spark.

The only person who doesn't seem to be affected by them is Neon. He bops round the room, singing and throwing out ideas for songs that he and I could sing together, but none of them feels right.

"How about 'Boulevard of Broken Dreams'?" he asks, pointing to the poster. "That's a good one."

I don't know the song. I'm not sure how Neon does.

Maybe Mr Ross has recommended him all that old punk-pop he likes so much.

"We can try it," I say, "but it sounds a bit depressing."

Neon takes a guitar down from the wall. "Yeah, maybe we need something more upbeat. Something that will get the crowd going."

I swallow and try to ignore the nerves gnawing at my stomach. I really need this to go well, especially since Neon has roped loads of people from school into coming on Saturday – more than will be able to fit in the bookshop, probably. It's not only that I want to prove to everyone who saw me chicken out the first time that I really can do it: I want to prove it to myself too.

"Why don't you just do 'Don't Stop Believin'?" Caitlin asks. "You guys practised so much for Friday Showcase, you might as well perform it again."

"I don't know." I sit on the desk beside Tilly, trying to block out the memory of all those faces staring at me as I hurried off the stage. "It might remind me of last time and make my nerves worse."

"That's true." Neon nods as he twirls the tuning pegs. "Plus, we don't want people to think we're a Journey cover band."

I take out my phone and go through my Favourites playlist for ideas. We try a few songs from musicals again, another couple that are constantly on the radio right now, but nothing seems to fit. I don't know if it's because of the Blanks, if they're sapping my ability to think outside the box, or if my nerves are getting in the way. But the longer we go without finding the right song, the further my confidence wanes.

"Maybe this is a bad idea." My shoulders slump as I slide my phone back into my pocket. "I'll probably croak like I did last time anyway."

"No!" Neon shouts. "You're going to be amazing. I can feel it."

Suddenly a loud scream rings through the corridor. Hannah glances round, but the rest of us don't even react. It's probably one of the younger kids mucking about. But then a high-pitched shriek is added to the first, and a third and a fourth, and then a chorus of heavy, rapid footsteps goes thundering past.

"Get out!" A teacher's voice, loud and panicked. "Everyone out, now!"

Tilly and I exchange wide-eyed looks and rush to the door. A wave of people go sprinting past, some screaming, some pale-faced with terror. I step outside and an ice-cold current of fear moves through my whole body. Standing at the other end of the corridor is an animal the size of a bull. It has the form of a wolf, but its eyes are red and its shaggy fur is the brownish green of muddied grass. Beside me, Tilly draws in a sharp breath.

"That's a cù-sìth," she whispers, pronouncing it 'coo-shee'. "It's a sign of death."

The animal paces in confused circles, growling and snapping its enormous jaws. The doors leading to the main hallway are shut, but I can hear panicked shouts behind them. Seeing the animal, Caitlin and Hannah scream and push past me into the corridor, then think better of it and duck back into the classroom to hide. Elsie tries to pull us inside so she can lock the door, but Neon shakes his head. "Dude, we can't let that thing roam around the school! It's going to scare people to death."

He takes a step towards the animal. The cù-sìth raises its head and growls, revealing yellowish fangs that make my breath catch in my throat. One of the Maths teachers, Mr Anghel, comes running down the corridor, his usually ruddy face almost green. He shouts at Neon to get back, but Neon keeps walking towards the cù-sìth. After days of inaction, my imagination finally kicks into gear. The end of this scene plays out before my eyes: Neon tackling a beast three times his size and being ripped to shreds outside the Home Economics classroom.

"You need to get out of here," Neon tells the cù-sìth, raising his voice to be heard above its snarls. "They don't know what you are. They'll kill you."

The beast snaps its jaws at Neon, but his words seem to get through: after a moment, it shrinks back against the wall, its growls fading to a whisper. Neon kneels down beside it and gingerly puts one hand on its snout. Mr Anghel's eyes are enormous behind his thick glasses, but he collects himself and hisses at us to follow him to the fire escape. Tilly ushers Jamie and Elsie out, then tells Caitlin and Hannah to follow, but I can't leave Neon.

"Time to go, buddy," he tells the creature. "You don't belong here."

Neon strokes the cù-sìth's snout. My heart leaps into my throat, but the animal lowers its head and closes its eyes. When it disappears, it's much more sudden than when the Blanks made the character in the park vanish yesterday. One minute it's there, and the next Neon's hand is stretched towards nothing but open air.

"That's it," says Neon, though the cù-sìth is no longer here to hear him. "Time to go."

~

The headteacher decides to close school for the rest of the day while they deal with the issue, though, by the time the animal-rescue team arrives, there's no trace of any wolf and the incident has morphed into a rumour. I call Carrie and ask her to come and pick Neon and me up a little early, and fifteen minutes later her yellow Beetle comes round the corner. I head towards it while Neon dawdles behind with Russell and Hari, who are asking him to retell the story of how he single-handedly faced down a wolf – they were at football practice and missed the whole thing.

"Hello, you!" Carrie's face breaks into a bright smile when she sees me. She leans across the car to open the passenger-side door. "Are you coming back with us?"

"If that's OK." I slide in beside her. "We really need to practise for our open-mic night on Saturday. We had a rehearsal at lunch, but it got cut short. We haven't even picked a song yet."

"Oh, Tamara has a huge record collection in the lounge. You're sure to find something in there." Carrie's eyes light up. "Do you need more acts? I'm happy to play a few tunes on my theremin if it'll help the bookshop."

I have no idea what a theremin is but, judging by our rehearsal, our event needs all the help it can get. "That would be great."

Neon runs through the school gates, his bag bumping against his back. He's almost at the car when Matt Lewis and a few other kids in our year shout his name.

He shoots Carrie an apologetic smile and hangs back to talk to them. Carrie smiles as she watches him jog along the pavement, holding his bag over his head to shield his hair from the rain.

"You know, it's been really nice getting to know Neon," she says softly. "I never wanted my own children. I'm not a baby person – far too much poop and crying for my liking. But I always liked the idea of having an older kid around. Someone I can have a proper conversation with."

"He likes you a lot," I say, smiling. "I think you remind him of his mum."

Carrie glances at me, her eyebrows raised. "So you based her character on me, is that what you're saying?"

"No! Well – maybe a bit."

"It wouldn't be the first time," Carrie says with a laugh. "Well, I'm flattered. I'm glad I can help you two out. I really do think you should talk to your mums about this, though. Monika's a writer, and Liv owns a bookshop. Surely, if anyone is going to understand, it'll be them."

Neon pulls open the door and climbs into the back seat. As Carrie drives off, a wave of exhaustion comes crashing over me. I lean back against the headrest, watching fat raindrops race down the windowpane while Neon fills Carrie in on what happened with the cù-sìth at school.

After a few streets, Carrie hits the brakes. I sit up, and my stomach flips when I see why she's stopped.

"That's them, isn't it?" Carrie raises a trembling finger. "The Blanks."

All I can do is nod. There are five of them this time. All different heights and body shapes, all wearing different clothes, but all exactly alike in their sad pale emptiness.

The barren ovals of their faces turn to us. One Blank takes a step towards the car, and then another. They know Neon is here. They sense it.

"What do we do?" I whisper.

Carrie shakes her head. "I don't know. I … I can't think."

Her face is changing. The light in her eyes fades; her mouth droops; her shoulders sag as she grips the steering wheel. It's like the personality is draining out of her. I don't understand it – I've been closer to the Blanks than she is now, and they've never affected me this badly.

"Carrie!" Neon gives her shoulder a light shake. "Think of Aurora, Carrie."

That brings some of the spark back into her eyes. Carrie looks at me, still frowning in confusion, but eventually gives a small nod. Outside, the Blanks are still advancing. Their arms rise and their hands reach towards us, the fingers as pale and thin as bones.

Carrie swallows. "They're not … *people*, are they? They're not alive?"

"No," Neon says in a low, tight voice. "They're nothing."

With that, Carrie slams her foot on the accelerator. The tyres squeal as the car races towards the Blanks. In the space of a few seconds, their colourless figures grow larger and larger, filling the entire windscreen. A second before the car comes into contact with them, they scatter into the darkness. When I look behind me, they're nowhere to be seen.

Twenty-nine

When I wake up the next morning, Tilly has sent me a video. It's a thirty-second clip showing a crowd of people on the beach at Chanonry Point on the Black Isle. It's a good place for spotting dolphins – when we had a picnic there for Mum's birthday last summer, there were dozens of people with binoculars or fancy cameras on tripods. But this crowd is something else: two hundred onlookers, maybe more, all talking excitedly and gazing out to sea. After a few seconds, there's a rumbling sound, the surface begins to tremble and a whale jumps out of the water.

A purple whale.

It's like a scene from a Disney film. The whale is *enormous* – impossibly big, way too big to be real – and its skin is the deep, sparkling amethyst of Aurora's eyes. On the shore, the people in the crowd gasp and clap and hold up their cameras. The whale twists elegantly in the air, gliding in a perfect arc against the pale grey sky, then slips back into the water with a splash.

The image is so dazzling, I press the video call button without thinking about the fact that Tilly and I haven't talked over the phone in years, and I don't know if we're at that stage of being friends again. Luckily it only rings twice before her face appears on the screen. She's still in bed – I recognise the teal-green duvet cover and the pile of plushies – with Bella tucked up beside her.

"What do you think?" Tilly skips the hellos, exactly like old times. "It's got to be another one, right? Everyone in the comments is saying the video is fake but I ran it through some websites that detect AI-generated content and they only rated it two per cent likely."

"Definitely from the Realm, then."

I sigh. My hair is a bird's nest, and my eyes are still smudged with yesterday's mascara, but Tilly's seen me looking much worse – like the time I tried to dye my hair red in primary seven.

"That beach is about thirty miles from here, though," I say. "What do you think it means that they're turning up further away?"

"No idea. But maybe it's a good thing!" Tilly sits up, sending a cat plushie sliding off the pile. "Maybe the Blanks will head over there and forget all about Neon. Huge purple whales have got to be more of a priority than one teenage boy who looks exactly like anyone else."

I tell her about the Blanks lingering outside school last night. Once we got back to the director's house, Carrie and Neon decided that it would best if he stayed away from school today. Whenever I've actually seen the Blanks, they've been in quiet or dark spots, and very few people have been around. They don't seem to like others to notice them, but if they want to get to Neon, they'll have to take that risk eventually. Our school isn't safe for him any more.

"So I was thinking I might have the flu today. Or maybe a stomach bug, or a migraine." I wince and press a hand to my forehead. "But also that I might suddenly feel much better after my mums go to the bookshop and I decide to cycle over to see Neon."

"Now you mention it, you look like you've got a migraine *and* a stomach bug *and* the flu. You should definitely stay off school." Tilly grins and lifts Bella's paw to wave goodbye. "But make sure you recover before the disco tonight. I need to see that costume!"

~

Two hours and one Oscar-worthy performance later, I arrive at the director's house on my bike. Aurora is lounging on the chaise longue, her coat glittering in the weak October sunlight. Neon is making crêpes, the food Karma would always make for him when he was feeling down. He doesn't seem to enjoy having to do it himself – he grumbles about not understanding British measurements, then cracks an egg so hard the entire shell shatters into the bowl. I help him pick out the pieces before taking the bowl from him.

"Here, I'll do it." I grab a wooden spoon from the worktop and begin mixing the ingredients together. "Are you OK? You seem a bit down."

"Yeah. Not the best day." Neon sinks on to a stool by the worktop. His head drops into his hands. "I loved your school. Being there made me feel, I dunno, actually real. It sucks I can't go any more."

"It might not be forever," I say. "You've been here for two weeks now, and the Blanks seem to have much more trouble finding you than the other characters."

"That's because everyone here believes I'm a normal person. The other characters don't have that, so they'll be easier to track down." He runs a finger through the flour on the worktop. "But I can't stay in this house forever, and I can't keep running from them."

"I really don't think they'll find you here. Maybe we could ask Tamara if you could stay a bit longer, even after they come back. There are so many rooms, I bet they'll…"

"Laurie." Neon looks up at me. His dark eyes are serious. He doesn't seem anything like the shooting star of a person I wrote into my story, or the carefree, happy kid I met at the train station two weeks ago. "I think it's time for me to go."

My heart plummets to the floor. "No. We'll sort this out. There has to be something we can do."

"There's not. I don't know why but my being here has obviously opened the door for a bunch of other characters to follow me into the real world. Look how people reacted to the cù-sìth yesterday. We can't have creatures like that wandering around." He looks at Aurora and swallows. "Besides, it'll bring more and more Blanks here, and you've seen what that's doing to everybody. I'll come to the Halloween disco tonight, but after that I'm going to leave. I want to do it before they get to me first."

Deep down, I know he's right. It's the safest option for everyone, the sensible option, but also the loneliest one. A lump fills my throat, and, before I can stop myself, tears are spilling down my cheeks. Neon moves round the worktop to give me a hug. He holds me for a long moment, then steps back and takes both of my hands in his.

"Promise me something." He ducks his head so his gaze meets mine. "Promise me that you'll sing at the open-mic night, even if I'm not there."

More tears well up in my eyes. I pull my hand away and force a laugh. "Come on. Don't be so dramatic."

"I'm serious! You can do it without me, Laurie. You always could."

I wipe my cheeks. I can't promise that because I still don't think it's true. "Well, if this is going to be your last day," I say, sniffing, "we have to make it a good one. No – the *best* one."

Neon's freckles shift with his smile. "I know where to start."

We finish making the crêpe mix and put it into the fridge to rest, then Neon leaves Aurora with a bunch of carrots and takes me through a door at the back of the house. It opens on to a small staircase, which leads down to something that makes my jaw drop: an underground swimming pool with a glass roof looking on to the garden. Small blue lights shine along the edge, making the water shimmer like satin.

"Carrie turned the heating on yesterday, but I haven't gone in yet," Neon says, dipping a toe in. "I wasn't sure how well I'd be able to swim in the real world, and I doubt Aurora is much of a lifeguard."

Neither of us have swimsuits, but Neon happily strips down to his boxers, and I jump in with my T-shirt on over my underwear. Neon does have some trouble adjusting to the water at first: the pressure is different in the Realm, and he takes a few minutes to work out how to keep himself afloat. I'm surprised he didn't dive in as soon as he saw the pool – the Neon I created would have done a cannonball into the water without a second thought.

But Neon isn't exactly the way I wrote him any more. He's becoming more layered, more complex. He's becoming a real person, with interests and reactions different to the ones I made up for him. I think about him talking about his 'purpose' coming here, like he was a plot device for my story. I don't want his time in this world to be all about that. This is his story too.

Soon Neon is swimming confidently, gliding through the water in a quick, neat front crawl. I do a few lengths, then lie on my back, my T-shirt blooming out around me like a jellyfish. It's started to rain, and the drops beat out a soothing pattern on the glass roof. At the back of the garden, the trees shake slightly in the wind; every so often, an orange or amber leaf flutters away and glides against the glass. Being here, floating in the warm water, all my worries drift away: the bookshop, the performance, even the Blanks.

After a few dozen lengths of the pool, Neon comes to join me. He rolls on to his back and lets out a happy sigh. I don't even remember the last time I went swimming. Mutti used to take me almost every weekend, but at some point I started worrying about what I looked like in my swimsuit and what the chlorine was doing to my hair, and we stopped. I hadn't realised how much I'd missed it.

We stay in the pool so long, our fingertips start to prune – something Neon finds fascinating. Afterwards, we help ourselves to super-soft robes and slippers from a set of shelves in the corner and go back upstairs to check on Aurora. She's fallen asleep on the chaise longue, tiny tinkling sounds leaving her mouth with every breath. I sit on the floor to watch her for a moment, marvelling at how strange and incredible these past two weeks have been. After a moment, Neon comes to sit beside me.

"I think she's ready to leave too," Neon whispers. "She loves you and Carrie and Tilly, but she needs to be with her own kind."

The lump in my throat bobs up again. I wish I could stop time, or go back to that Saturday at the train station and relive it all over again. I look at Neon, taking in the freckles on his cheeks, the drops of water rolling off his curls. Caitlin's voice fills my mind. *Kiss him, kiss him. Oh my God, you're hopeless.*

I have to do this – before I lose my nerve yet again, before the Blanks reach us. Before Neon leaves forever.

Drawing in a quick breath, I lean towards Neon. His eyes meet mine, startled at first, then understanding. I pause for a moment, waiting for him to tell me this is OK. He gives the tiniest nod and moves towards me until our lips touch. This is it – it's finally happening. The lie I told all those months ago has finally come to life.

I'd always worried that I wouldn't know how to kiss someone, that I'd bash my teeth against the other person's, or my tongue would take on a life of its own. In fact it's easy. It doesn't even feel that awkward. Neon and I know each other so well, and we fall straight into a rhythm, just like when we sing together.

But somehow it's not like I expected, either. I'm not sure what I thought would happen – not fireworks or fanfare, obviously, but something more than this. Some shift inside me that would make me feel different. More grown-up.

Instead there's nothing. I don't feel different. I don't feel much at all.

"Sorry." I pull away, and my cheeks instantly flush. "Sorry – I don't know why I—"

"That's OK." Neon presses his lips together. "That was kind of weird, huh?"

"Yeah." I swallow. "I don't know why, though."

"There could be lots of reasons." Neon shrugs. "Maybe we're not into each other like that. Maybe you don't feel ready to kiss anybody yet. Or maybe you're not interested in kissing anyone. Some people aren't, and that's OK."

Any one of those feels very plausible right now. I know that I probably wouldn't think about kissing so much if it wasn't for Caitlin and Hannah. They made me feel like a loser for never having done it, babyish for not having really thought about it before. But when I actually imagined kissing someone … there was never much push. It doesn't seem gross like it did when I was little, but it also doesn't give me butterflies. Neon could be right – maybe kissing boys isn't for me, or maybe I'm not into the idea of kissing anyone. I just don't know.

"Maybe," I say slowly. "I can't decide."

To my surprise, tears start to prickle at my eyes. Ever since I met them, Caitlin and Hannah have seemed so sure of who they are and who they like. They seem so ready to be grown up, and I don't think I am yet. I know everyone is different, and everyone changes in their own time, but they make me feel like I'm losing a race I never wanted to run.

"You don't have to decide anything," Neon says gently. "It's cool some people know what they like when they're this young, but it's not like that for everyone."

I nod. Mutti told me that she knew she was a lesbian when she was twelve, but Mum didn't come out until she was in her twenties. I think of Tilly, the rainbow pin on her jacket. I wonder if she knew she was pan all this time and never told me. It's nothing for me to be annoyed about – it wasn't my business. But we talked about everything back then. I hope she didn't feel like she had to hide it, if she did know.

"Do you know?" I ask Neon.

Thinking about it, I realised I never properly thought about whether Neon was straight or bi or anything else. He may have started out as a fictional first kiss, but all he was to me was a friend. I never made him talk about girls or anyone else he might have liked. All I wanted was a proper friend.

He laughs. "If I know, it's only because you decided that I should know."

I shake my head. "No, that's not true. You're here now. You can decide that for yourself."

"Then … we don't know together. Cool." Neon grins and jumps to his feet. "How about those crêpes now? I want to eat all the real-world food I can physically stomach before I have to leave."

Thirty

'Monster Mash' is playing full blast when I arrive at school for the Halloween disco that evening. The gym is covered with pumpkin fairy lights, bunting shaped like bats and ghosts, and there are fake cobwebs hanging from the tables of drinks and snacks. In the middle of the space, three characters from *Doctor Who* are dancing. Thirteen (Tilly) and Six (Jamie) are doing something that looks like a slow-motion duel with invisible lightsabres while Twelve (Elsie) is spinning around to show off the red lining of her coat. Already laughing, I run over to join them. Twelve-aka-Elsie screams when she sees me.

"No way! You're Callan! Tilly wouldn't tell us what you were coming as. She wanted it to be a surprise."

After an hour of searching and raiding my wardrobe and Joel's the other day, Tilly and I finally came up with a costume for me: the lead character from *Shadows of the Sea*, the sea-monster boy-band novel that we both love. We sliced up an old black shirt of Joel's, I borrowed Mutti's black skinny jeans, then she and Mum spent ages after tea tonight painting my hands and face bright blue. I'm probably going to look like a Smurf for the next few days.

"Tilly's idea," I say, grinning at her. "Hey, are you two OK? I didn't get a chance to talk to you after the rehearsal yesterday."

I thought the disco might be quieter than usual after the cù-sìth's appearance – that some kids wouldn't want to risk coming to school after a giant wolf had been on the loose, or that their parents wouldn't let them out of the house. But Jamie and Elsie just blink in confusion and ask what I mean. Tilly says something about needing some more lemonade and drags me to the drinks table.

"They don't remember," she whispers. "I don't think anybody does! No one mentioned it at school all day."

The creature's snarling, snapping jaws flash into my head. The memory makes goosebumps ripple over my blue-painted arms.

"How could they forget about something like that?"

"Maybe people forget after the character goes back to the Realm?" Tilly shrugs. "It must be different for you and me because we know the truth about where they came from. That's the only explanation I can think of."

So, after Neon leaves, everyone else is going to forget about him. I'll be able to talk to Joel and Carrie and Tilly about him, but nobody else. Caitlin and Hannah will forget him, and about their apology for doubting me. Hari and Russell and Mr Ross and all his other fans won't have any memory of hearing him sing. Neon has made so many connections here, so quickly, and after a few days or weeks they're all going to disappear.

"Where is Neon?" I ask Tilly. "Is he here yet?"

She points to the opposite side of the hall where someone wearing a bird mask and toilet paper loosely wrapped round their body is talking to two Hulks. I wander over, tap Neon on the shoulder, then duck down behind a row of chairs. When I jump back up to scare him, Neon's eyes light up behind the mask.

"Awesome costume!" He pushes his mask up for a better look. "You've done Callan proud."

"Thanks." I wait until the Hulks – Hari and Russell – are out of earshot, then whisper, "No sign of the Blanks?"

Neon shakes his head. "Not that I've noticed. Maybe they're too busy chasing down that whale."

By now, the video that Tilly sent me this morning has spread all over the internet. Most people still don't believe it's real – a big science organisation even released a debunking video about how sparkling purple whales definitely don't exist – but, when I rewatched it this afternoon, there were a lot of comments from people who seemed totally convinced.

"There's no point in worrying about it," Neon says with a smile and a shrug. "What's going to happen is going to happen. Let's just have fun tonight."

We go to join Tilly and the others, who are now slow-dancing to an upbeat pop song. Caitlin and Hannah arrive together a few minutes later. Hannah is wearing a white dress with fairy wings and a wonky gold halo over her head, and Caitlin is head-to-toe in red with plastic devil horns. I go to say hi, and we all say how great we look in our costumes – Caitlin doesn't even make any snide remarks about mine being weird, so she must be in a good mood.

"Are you feeling better?" she asks. "Tilly said you were ill. You didn't text us or anything."

She looks slightly hurt, and I'm surprised. It shouldn't

be surprising that the people I consider my best friends are sad that I've decided to take a step back from them. But that's the problem, especially with Caitlin. I never know where I stand: if today will be a day she likes me or a day I'm the butt of the joke.

"I'm fine," I say. "I feel much better now."

We talk a while longer but soon I find myself drifting over to dance with the *Doctor Who* trio again. We have another dance-off, all pulling the most ridiculous moves we can think up. I catch Caitlin and Hannah looking over at us from across the room a couple of times. Caitlin's smile is bordering on a cringe, but Hannah looks like she wants to join in.

When 'Time Warp' comes on, I rush over and grab her hands. "Come and dance!" I shout over the music. "You love *Rocky Horror*!"

For a moment, it looks like she's going to say yes, but then she glances at Caitlin and shakes her head. I really hope Caitlin starts being nicer to her. But, if not, I hope Hannah realises she deserves a better best friend too.

The disco goes on, and it feels exactly like any other. Two girls from my Maths class have an argument and one leaves crying. A fourth-year boy throws up in the corner, and no one believes him when he insists all he's drunk is Coke. Hari and Neon have a dance-off to a song called 'Monster', and they surprise everybody by being really good – Neon knows the entire routine off by heart. That's not something I wrote into his story. It's all him.

But, some time after nine o'clock, the atmosphere suddenly shifts. The volume of the music doesn't change, but the sound becomes dulled in my ears. The colours of the costumes around me fade. I look down at my own bright blue hands, the paint now rubbed away from my palms and fingertips, and hardly remember the story that inspired my costume.

When I turn round, fear fizzes through every cell in my body.

Six Blanks stand in the doorway to the gym, their pale figures silhouetted by the strip lights in the corridor. No, more than six – eight, ten – all dressed in those familiar colourless clothes, ambling into the room like zombies. Their heads turn slowly around the space, searching for something they can't see or hear but can sense around them. A strange atmosphere seeps into the room: a dull, hollow feeling, like a million bad days rolled into this one moment.

Behind them, two first-year girls dressed as superheroes are frozen with fear: one bursts into tears, and the other grabs her friend's hand and pulls her down the corridor. Other people have noticed the Blanks too, but they seem more confused or impressed than scared – it hasn't occurred to them that what they're seeing could be anything other than a costume.

Beside me, Russell drops his cup of lemonade. "Whoa! Who is that? They're creepy as hell!"

One of the Blanks takes a step forward and begins to move towards the centre of the hall where Neon is dancing with Tilly and Elsie. The others follow, a slow-moving army heading for their target. The fog is already rolling into my mind in thick waves. If they come much closer, I won't be able to think properly at all.

I rush through the crowd and grab Neon's hand. He

turns to me with a big smile on his face, but it disappears when he sees the faceless figures heading towards us.

"They're here!" I shout. "We have to go. Now!"

Neon doesn't move. His eyes are fixed on the Blanks slowly edging across the dance hall, a mixture of fear and defiance in his expression. Elsie and Jamie look from us to the Blanks, obviously confused, but unable to find the words to ask what's going on.

Tilly straightens her short blond wig and swallows. "I'll try to slow them down," she says. "You guys get out of here."

I don't want Tilly to stay, but there's no time to argue with her. I drag Neon across the gym, through the fire escape and out into the street. We run past the bakery, along the park and towards my house. Neon pulls his hand away and shouts at me to stop, but I ignore him and keep running – I need to get him away from those things as quickly as possible.

When we turn a corner on to the high street, I skid to a halt. This part of town would usually be deserted at this time of night, but now it's filled with figures. They linger by the bus stop, drift past the post office, stand in clusters in shop doorways. My heart skips a beat, then thunders even faster than before. Standing between us and safety are dozens, maybe even hundreds, of Blanks.

Thirty-one

As the Blanks sense Neon's presence, a wave of movement washes over the street. One by one, they spin towards us, an entire crowd of empty faces turned in our direction. Breathing fast, I try to imagine a way out of this. Nothing comes. I close my eyes and squeeze the top of my nose, but the fog in my head won't clear. After a moment, I feel a hand on my shoulder.

"Laurie, my time's up," Neon says softly. "If I go back to the Realm now, they won't have the chance to erase me."

"No!" I shake my head. "No, there has to be a way."

"But look how many of them there are! If I stay, they're going to suck the imagination out of everyone in this town."

I think about it: Mutti not being able to write; me unable to come up with my stories; Tilly without her love of all things fantastical; Carrie taking down the unicorn ornaments on her mantelpiece, hiding them away in the attic; no one in our town making music or drawing or creating beautiful things. The idea is too sad for words.

But so is the thought of letting Neon go. I'm still not ready to give up yet.

I scan the street. The lights are on in Every Book & Cranny. Deep in the mist of my mind, there's a tiny spark of hope. I reach for Neon's sleeve and pull him towards the shop. Some of the Blanks stumble in our direction as we run down the street. The fog in my head thickens, but they're too slow to catch us.

Inside the shop, Mum and Mutti sit together by the computer, mugs in their hands, their foreheads creased with frowns. Joel is cross-legged on the floor, rearranging the cookbooks. When I hammer on the door, they all jump; Mutti's tea sloshes over the rim of her cup and on to her cream cardigan.

Joel leaps to his feet and hurries to the entrance. My heart flutters as he undoes the double locks and opens the door. "What's wrong? Has something happened?" He reaches for me as I pull Neon inside, his eyes widening when he finally notices the Blanks swarming the high street. "What are *those*?"

I slam the door shut and bolt it closed again. Mum and Mutti rush over from the counter. Mum's face is pale, and Mutti barely seems to have noticed the beige splodge on her favourite cardigan. They both look so worried, and for a moment all I feel is regret. I should have told them what was going on much sooner. We're in over our heads, and now I don't know even know where to start.

"Don't worry." Neon holds up his hands with a wobbly smile. "Everything's OK. It's just…"

"Everything is not OK! Those *things* are after Neon. He needs to get out of here now." I run to the storeroom and grab Mum's car keys from the hook behind the door. "He's been staying at Carrie's friend's house – you know,

Tamara Mackenzie, the director? They live in that big house in the woods. Can you drive us there? Please?"

Mutti and Mum look at each other. There are times when my parents appear to have an entire conversation in one glance, but right now they both look completely flummoxed.

Mutti turns back to us and shakes her head in confusion. "Wait – start again, Laurie. Those people are after Neon?" She peers at the Blanks through the window, more confused than worried. "Who are they?"

"And what do you mean, Neon's been staying at Tamara Mackenzie's house?" Mum says, a hint of anger creeping into her words. "Does Carrie know that?"

"Yes, it was her idea, but – look, there's no time to explain!" I shake the keys in frustration. The Blanks are drawing in, and the fog in my head is expanding. "I promise I'll tell you everything later. Please can you trust me on this?"

Joel rubs his forehead. He seems to be having trouble thinking too, but he takes the keys from me. "I can drive you over there."

"No, we're coming," Mum says, snatching them back from him. "It sounds like we've got things to talk to Carrie about."

While Joel locks up the shop, the rest of us hurry out through the back door and down the side street where my parents' car is parked. Mum slides into the driver's seat and Mutti gets in beside her, rubbing her temples like she's getting a headache.

Joel appears a moment later and squeezes into the back beside Neon and me. "Is this something to do with Aurora?"

he asks, pulling the door shut behind him. "Is she OK?"

"Who's Aurora?" Mum glances at me as she slowly manoeuvres out of her parking space. When none of us replies, she sighs. "Fine. Maybe Carrie will give us some answers."

She edges down the narrow street and turns left on to a wider residential road. A group of seven or eight-year-olds dressed as cartoon characters come out of a house, each clutching a plastic pumpkin full of sweets. Suddenly one stops by the gate and drops his haul. As chocolate bars and monkey nuts go tumbling on to the pavement, a Blank glides past. The pale sphere where its face should be turns slowly towards the children. Half of them freeze; the others scream and sprint back into the house.

"What are those faceless people supposed to be?" Mutti turns her head to stare at the Blanks as we drive past. "Are they from one of those superhero movies?"

Mum points to the other side of the street. "Look, there's another one."

Under a street lamp, a second Blank is walking slowly towards a man dressed in a medieval-style tunic. The headlights of Mum's car wash over them, making the Blank's featureless face glow like the moon. As I twist round in my seat, the Blank puts its hand on the man's chest. He crumbles into a thousand tiny pieces and falls to the ground like ashes, blown away on the wind. I gasp and clamp my hand over my mouth, but my parents are looking ahead and didn't see the character vanish into nothing.

As we drive, more Blanks appear. They seem to come from nowhere, pale flames springing into the night air. I keep waiting for Mum or Mutti to realise that this isn't normal, that there's something very strange going on here. But, like the kids at school, they don't seem to have considered anything other than the most logical explanation. Soon they stop asking questions and sit in silence, their expressions turning blank like Carrie's did yesterday. It's as if all their curiosity about the situation has run out.

As Mum turns on to the long road that borders the loch, a cacophony of horns and raised voices fills the air. The traffic on both sides of the road has come to a standstill. Some cars seem to have been abandoned, doors still gaping open. Mum stops the car behind a furiously honking minivan. Neither she nor Mutti comments on what's going on, so Joel gets out to take a look.

"There seems to have been an accident, but I can't see anything," he says. "Can't hear any ambulances on their way, either."

Neon and I climb out of the back seat after him. Down by the water, a constellation of lights twinkles. At first I think it's a boat, but when my eyes adjust to the dim light I realise it's coming from the banks of the loch. A large crowd of people have gathered there, and they're all holding phones or cameras to the water, just like in the video that Tilly sent me this morning. In the darkness, the surface of the water ripples. Someone screams, and I can't tell whether it's from fear or excitement.

Neon takes a sharp breath. "Hang on. You don't think…?"

It takes me a long moment for the mist in my mind to clear and for me to understand what he's suggesting. There's something in the water.

Something is moving in Loch Ness.

Thirty-two

Before I can stop him, Neon runs towards the crowd. I race after him, ignoring my parents' confused questions. The crowd by the shore is bigger than I realised, and quickly growing: dozens of people rush down the banks after us, some shouting into phones, others narrating what they see as they film. Neon pushes through them and arrives at the water's edge. A few metres away, a movement makes the surface ripple. There are more screams; a woman carrying a giant camera wades right into the water to get a better shot.

"We need to go back to the car," I tell Neon. "If that's what I think it is, the Blanks will be on their way. You saw how many of them there are now."

"Dude, the road's completely gridlocked. We're not getting out of there for hours."

A large shape slips past the surface and flicks water towards the crowd. It's too dark to make out what it is, and it quickly disappears back into the depths of the loch. Someone behind me says it's only a big fish, maybe a water snake. Other people – probably those who haven't been around the Blanks and are still able to imagine something more fantastical – take this as proof of what they've suspected.

"Nessie!" An older man in a green coat punches the air. "I *knew* you were real, girl!"

More and more people arrive, and the crowd jostles as the newcomers push to the front for a better view. Behind us, someone calls my name. I turn round to see my mums and Joel making their way towards the loch. Nudging Neon to follow me, I squeeze past two people with their phones held up at arm's length and go to join my family. My parents still looked dazed, but Joel has an ear-to-ear grin on his face.

"Did you see it?" He stands on his tiptoes for a better look at the water. "Is it really her?"

Mum shakes her head in confusion. "Laurie, *what* are you doing? Why are we here?"

I point to the loch and swallow. "I think, uh ... I think that's the Loch Ness Monster in there."

My parents stare at us, then at each other, then at me and Neon again. Mum scoffs and says that's impossible, that it's only a story. But there is, finally, the tiniest hint of wonder in Mutti's eyes. She fixes Neon with a long gaze, her eyebrows furrowed in a frown.

"Who *are* you?" she asks. "Where did you come from?"

An excited scream from somewhere in the crowd saves us from answering. A huge group of people in costumes come rushing down the path, including three Doctors, two Hulks, an angel and a devil who have walked here from school. Tilly makes a beeline for me, with the others right behind her. They all look totally bewildered, especially Caitlin. She heads for the water with her phone held high, but it seems to be more of a reflex than out of curiosity about what everyone is trying to film. Hannah follows with the same blank-eyed look, her halo lopsided and her angel wings hanging down at her elbows. Mum and Mutti exchange panicked expressions, then hurry after them, shouting something about being careful not to fall in.

"Are you all OK?" Neon asks Tilly. His eyes flit over Russell and Hari's smudged green faces as they follow the girls towards the loch. "Where are the Blanks?"

"We trapped some of them in the gym until you guys had escaped. They managed to get out and headed for the high street. There are *so* many of them now." Tilly blinks hard, as if trying to clear the fog in her head. "Everyone's saying there's something in the water. Is it true?"

Neon nods. "There's definitely something, and if it's really Nessie, I think I need to take her back. There are way too many people here. I don't want her – or anybody else – to get hurt."

"What do you mean, take her back?" Jamie asks, frowning. "Take her back to where?"

While Tilly and Neon try to come up with an explanation, I turn back to the loch. More people have gone into the water now, willing to risk being attacked or getting hypothermia for a good shot of one of the world's most famous monsters. Neon is right. This could end really, really badly.

"OK," I tell him. "You should do it."

"I don't know if I'll be able to convince her to go by herself, like I did with the cù-sìth. I might need to leave too." Neon bites his lip. "Actually I'm going to go back either way. The Blanks won't be far away now. I don't have much time."

My throat goes tight, and my eyes sting, but I manage to nod and say OK again. Neon holds out his arms and I step into them, letting him wrap me in a tight hug. I close my eyes and try to remember what it's like to have him here, in the real world with me. I want to tell him how grateful I am for the past two weeks. For saving me from being humiliated at the train station, for showing me that I deserve better than the way Caitlin and Hannah treat me, for bringing me and Tilly back together. For being my friend.

But, before I say anything, the words evaporate from my mind. The chatter from the crowd dims. Some people spin round, dazed and frowning, searching for the reason for the sudden change in the air. When I follow their gazes, my breath catches and my heart clenches.

We're too late. The Blanks are already here.

~

The Blanks weave through the cars and walk slowly down the bank towards the loch, their empty faces turned to the water. My first instinct is to hide Neon. I grab his hand and pull him away from the crowd, behind a scattering of pine trees between the water's edge and the road. Tilly, Jamie and Elsie hurry after us, and the four of us crouch in a semicircle to shield Neon from view. After a moment, he lets out a muffled laugh.

"Thanks, guys, but this won't help," he says. "The Blanks can't see. They're still going to be able to sense me here."

I try to think of an alternative, but my mind is filled with mist. The Blanks keep coming, dozens and dozens of them slowly marching across the grass and into the crowd.

My heart pounds as we wait for one to finally come our way, but it doesn't happen. They step straight into the loch, walking in straight lines until their heads dip beneath the surface. Jamie takes out her phone to film the scene, then lets out a small cry of surprise. The camera only captures the crowd and the faint ripples of light on the dark surface of the loch. The Blanks don't show up at all.

One by one, the faceless figures disappear into the water. Even though I know they're not human, that they don't need to breathe like we do, it's unsettling to see their heads slip below the surface and out of sight. The loch ripples and bubbles, and at one point another shadowy shape pierces through the water, showering the crowd with droplets. But eventually Loch Ness falls still. Whatever was in there has vanished along with the Blanks.

Slowly, like sun breaking through the clouds, the fog in my brain lifts and I can think clearly again. Jamie and Elsie blink and stretch, as if waking up from a dream. Neon gets up and holds out his hands to help Tilly and me to our feet.

"Have they gone?" I clutch at Neon's hand. It's warm and clammy and *here*. Still here. "I think they've gone."

Confusion ripples over the crowd. Some people keep filming the water, hoping for another glimpse of whatever was in there, but most are already wandering away. Mutti and Mum come back towards us with Caitlin, Hannah, Russell and Hari, all of them asking a hundred questions at the same time. I look at Neon. He rubs at the birthmark above his eyebrow, a small, hopeful smile tugging at the corners of his mouth.

But then I feel it: the fog again, trickling past my ears

and into my mind. Tilly sucks in a breath and grabs my arm.

"Laurie – look."

One single Blank stands at the top of the grassy bank. Its smudged white face turns towards Neon. Its right arm lifts, and the colourless sleeve of its coat falls back to show a skeletal wrist and hand. It takes a step forward and the crowd parts to let it through. A couple of younger kids begin to cry, but most people stare at it with mild confusion. When it comes towards us, Mutti and Mum move instinctively in front of me, both stammering questions about what it wants. The Blank stops a few steps away from us. I've never been so close to one before. The mist in my mind swirls, growing thicker until the memory of the past few hours is a blur.

"Laurie?" Neon asks. "Are you OK?"

For a moment, I almost feel like I'm looking at a stranger. His face is familiar, the dark eyes and his freckles, but I can't remember spending time together. I try to grasp at memories of him, but it all fades into nothing.

Then Neon frowns, making the birthmark pinch above his eyebrow. I remember adding that light brown shape to his profile picture all those months ago, and suddenly the memories of the last two weeks come tumbling back. I can't let this thing erase him. Maybe he can't stay here but I can't let him be wiped from my mind, or Tilly's, or Hari's, or any of the other people who he's brought so much joy to in the past couple of weeks.

And then, like a lighthouse flickering in the distance, it comes to me: a way to keep Neon alive, at least in my head.

"There was once a boy called Neon," I say out loud.

"He lived in New York City. He loved music. He had a dog named Cauliflower."

Closing my eyes, I work my way back to the story I started to write in April. The details are so hazy, and for a long moment I stand speechless in front of the Blank, grasping for words that won't come. Flashes of imagined scenes flicker into my head. Neon sitting on the steps of a brownstone building, fiddling with a keyring while he waits for a friend. Neon making himself scrambled eggs in an apartment with skyscraper views, music playing in the background.

Slowly it all falls into place: Neon's glamorous life in a city I've never been to; seeing the world with his mum; forming a band with his friends. I haven't thought about that first version of Neon's story for a long time, but some of my feelings around it come back as I talk – how amazing it was to have a different person's world to dip into. The Blank is still right in front of me, the fear still hammers in my chest, but I try to let myself get swept away by the story, like I have in so many others.

After a minute, I feel an arm brush against mine. Tilly's voice rings out beside me. "Callan Campbell was the lead singer of a band called Cyanize – but that's not all he was."

She tells the story of *Shadows of the Sea*, reciting full paragraphs off by heart. Her words are high-pitched and trembling, but I feel her love for the story and its characters in them. Our voices overlap, the stories twirling round each other in the cold night air. And amazingly it seems to be doing something. The Blank is frozen, its pale fingers trembling centimetres away from us, but coming no further.

After a moment, the others join in too. Jamie and Elsie

choose episodes of *Doctor Who*, weaving tales of planets and time travel, aliens and weeping angels. Hannah tells the story of *Les Misérables*, Caitlin mumbles something about the plot of *Six*. Mum talks about her favourite Jane Austen book, Mutti about the characters in her next novel. Hari and Russell stumble over to us and, though they look completely baffled, join in: Hari launches into the backstory to one of his video games; Russell describes the comics that he's collected for years. Joel performs a Shakespearean monologue and, from what I can hear over all the ruckus, he's brilliant.

A few strangers even wander over and tell their own tales – tentatively at first, then more quickly and confidently as they get carried away by the plot. Soon the air around us is thick with stories. Behind the words are echoes of a thousand emotions: the shock of a great twist; the frustration of a brilliant cliffhanger; laughter and tears and sparks of understanding. There's the power of feeling seen, and the power of viewing the world through another person's eyes. The power of connecting with those who came before us, and the power of being transported to another world for a while.

And together it's too much for the Blank to push through. The ghostly white sphere of its face grows dimmer and dimmer, until it becomes translucent enough to make out the road and trees behind it. Like clouds parting, the strange atmosphere hanging over the loch finally clears. The beige clothes fall to a crumpled pile on the muddy ground. With a gasp from the crowd around us, the last of the Blanks disappears.

Thirty-three

It takes a long time for the traffic by the loch to clear. Word about the maybe-monster in the water has spread and people keep arriving, hoping to catch a glimpse of whatever was in there. Hordes of parents come to pick up the kids who came here from the disco too. My mums wait until Hannah's dad and Elsie's parents have managed to edge through the gridlock to take them and the others home, then let Neon, Joel, Tilly and me squash into the back of their car and drive us to Tamara's. Mum and Mutti both seem slightly shell-shocked. They keep starting to ask questions, then stopping halfway through the sentence, shaking their heads in bewilderment.

"You four," Mum says eventually, "have a lot of explaining to do."

~

After an hour and a half, our car eventually edges out of the traffic jam and on to the road towards Tamara's house. There don't seem to be any more characters from the Realm around, or at least not obvious ones like the vampire or the cù-sìth. And the whole time we don't see a single Blank.

"I really think they've all gone," I whisper to Neon. "I can't feel them any more."

Neon tells me he can't, either. Something about him is different now. As the light from the street lamps glides across the car, I spot two moles beneath his left ear that I've never noticed. There are a couple of small spots on his cheek, and the skin on his lower lip is slightly dry. It's like I'm seeing him in higher definition than before.

When we arrive at the director's house, Carrie comes out to the front step to meet us. She's wearing a lime-green dressing gown and there's an eye mask pushed up into her tousled red hair. "What's all this I hear about Nessie making an appearance in the loch?" she asks, yawning.

"We're not actually sure it was her." Neon runs up the steps to give her a hug. "There was definitely something, but it was too dark to see what it was. You didn't miss much."

"Oh, I'm not worried about that. I met Nessie in 1998. I was eating a tuna mayo sandwich by the loch and she popped up." Carrie turns to my parents. Seeing their baffled expressions, she laughs and gives Mum's arm an encouraging rub. "You two must have some questions, eh? Come on in. I'll make some tea."

She leads us through the hallway – Joel gasps when he sees Tamara's collection of awards – and into the kitchen. The moment they step inside, Mum screams and Mutti swears in German. Aurora is curled up on the floor, silk pillows beneath her, chomping on a carrot.

I slap a hand to my forehead. "Sorry. Should have warned you about her." I kneel down and stroke her mane to say hello. "This is Aurora. She's a unicorn."

"I … can see that." Mum sinks on to a stool by the breakfast island and grips the edge for balance. "OK. I think I'm ready to hear what's going on now."

As Carrie makes tea and toast, we finally tell my parents the whole story of how Neon came to be, and how he came to be here. Their eyes spark with questions, and probably a lot of doubts, but they listen in silence through our explanation of the Realm, finding Aurora, dodging the Blanks, until we reach the scene at the loch.

"Well." Mutti lets out a high-pitched laugh. "I'm officially not the most successful writer in our family. People say I'm good at bringing characters to life, but this is another level, Laurie."

"So what are you going to do now?" Mum asks Neon. "Are you still going to go back to this Realm place?"

"I don't know if I can any more." Neon swallows and shoots me a guilty look. "I actually tried while you were telling your stories, before the Blank disappeared. I was scared it would wipe me out, and it felt like my last chance to leave on my own terms. But, when I tried to do it, nothing happened."

Hope flutters in my stomach. "Do you think that means you're actually real now?"

"I think so?" Neon gives a small smile. "I guess it means I'm stuck here, either way."

"What about the Blanks?" Tilly asks. "If you're stuck here, does that mean they won't come after you?"

"I think so. When you told those stories and made the Blank disappear, it changed something. It's hard to explain, but I feel different than I did before. More … solid." Neon puts his hands to his cheeks, patting the contours

214

of his face like he's checking for changes. "I can't be totally sure, but something has changed. I think I'm properly, actually *real* now."

With screams of delight, Tilly and I both leap at Neon. Carrie comes over and wraps her arms round the three of us, then decides this calls for a celebration and goes to find something fun to eat in the cupboards. She comes back a moment later with a bottle of pink lemonade and more carrots for Aurora.

"I'm happy for you, Neon," Mum says with an uncertain smile. "But that means you're a minor with no parent or guardian responsible for you."

"Well, you know." Carrie clears her throat and twists the bottle cap. Her cheeks have turned the same shade as the lemonade. "Neon's very welcome to stay with me. My house isn't as fancy as this place, but I've got a spare room. You could do it up however you liked, make it your own."

Neon asks if she's serious. When Carrie says of course, his whole face lights up with happiness and he leaps up to hug her again. My cheeks are starting to hurt from smiling. Neon's very own home – and right next door to mine. This is more than I ever, ever could have hoped for.

Mum still isn't totally convinced. She points out that Neon will need paperwork if he wants a normal life here. He'll need a birth certificate to sign up for school, apply for a passport or learn to drive one day, and Carrie will have to register as a foster parent if he's going to stay with her long-term. Carrie says she has a friend in MI5 who owes her a favour and will be able to sort Neon out with all the papers. It's classified, of course, so she can't tell us the details.

Joel leans towards me. "That's a first," he whispers, grinning.

As I bite back a laugh, an idea comes to me. "Come on – I want to show you something."

While Carrie and my mums are discussing arrangements with Neon, and Tilly fusses over Aurora, I lead Joel back into the hallway. We admire Tamara Mackenzie's table full of awards for a while, then I take him upstairs to show him the framed film posters lining the landing. Actors stare out from the images. Some famous, some not so famous, but all part of Tamara's stories.

"I know it's hard, but I think you should try being an actor," I tell Joel. "I heard your monologue back at the loch there – you're really good. You should give it a go, if it's still what you want to do."

Joel bites his lip, his eyes still on a poster of a period drama that won Tamara a BAFTA in 2012. "Funny you should say that because I made a decision yesterday. I'm not going back to uni."

He lets out a sigh of relief, like saying it aloud has taken some of the weight off his shoulders. Joel and I aren't the hugging sort of siblings, but I hold my hand up to give him a high five. He smiles and, for the first time in ages, my brother looks like his old self again.

"Good," I say. "You don't seem happy there."

"Yeah, I'm really not. It's not for me at all." He looks at the next poster. "I don't know if acting is the answer, though. Success stories like Tamara are really rare, especially for people who don't have connections in the industry. But I'm going to join the theatre group in Inverness, get back into it. There you go. Now you're acting, Greg!"

For a second, I have no clue what he's talking about or who Greg is, but then I realise Joel's quoting one of the films he used to watch on repeat a few years ago. I come up with another line, and Joel bats back a third from a different film. When Neon comes upstairs a few moments later, he finds us cracking up between lines from *Sharknado*.

"You two are weird." He swats my ponytail and heads off to the eighties room. "I need to get my stuff. I'm staying at Carrie's tonight."

I help Neon pack his few belongings into his schoolbag and strip the bedsheets for Carrie to wash before Tamara comes home. It's past one o'clock now, but we're both too hyper and excited by everything that's happened tonight to feel tired. For the first time since the Blanks arrived, my mind feels sharp and clear again. Neon puts on a record from Tamara's collection while we tidy, and every line sparkles like a disco ball inside my head.

When we arrive back downstairs, Carrie and my mums are tidying the kitchen while Joel and Tilly lead Aurora out to the garden. Though none of us have said so, we all know it's time to say goodbye to her. She's not safe here. If she was ever discovered, she'd likely be kidnapped by some sort of authorities. We'd have to explain where we found her, and no one would ever believe the answer. She'd end up in a zoo, or bought by a billionaire as a pet for his kids. She needs to be free, and that means letting her go.

Outside, Carrie flicks a switch by the door. The trees lining the back of the lawn light up with hundreds of twinkling fairy lights. Aurora trots across the grounds, her coat and mane shimmering in the gentle light, then settles down at the foot of an apple tree. Carrie sits down on one side of her and strokes her mane.

"Thank you for coming, girl," she says softly. "It's been the highlight of my life, getting to meet you. And I once took a gravity-free flight with two members of the original cast of *The Addams Family*, so that's saying something."

Tilly sits down on Aurora's other side and gently caresses her back. "I think she's ready."

Mum and Mutti stroke Aurora's mane, both of them still too shocked to say much, then Joel and I take a moment to say goodbye. Neither Neon, Tilly or I have any photos of Aurora — we were all too worried that someone would find them and ask questions. But now I take one: Aurora curled up on the grass, Neon's and Tilly's arms draped across her back. Her coat and horn glow even in the picture, surrounding her with a white haze that makes the photo look fuzzy. No one else who saw this would think it was real. But we'll remember.

Neon crouches down and puts his hands on either side of Aurora's muzzle. He leans in to whisper something to her, then presses his face gently against hers. Aurora's amethyst eyes close, and she lets out one last tinkly whinny. Then, without a sound, she vanishes.

Thirty-four

I sleep so long that, by the time I wake up, my shift at Every Book & Cranny has already started. It sounds like my mums and Joel have gone to the shop: the house is completely quiet until someone begins knocking at the front door. I hurry downstairs in my pyjamas and find Neon standing on the front step, wearing a wide smile and a Glastonbury 97 T-shirt that he must have borrowed from Carrie.

"Hey, neighbour." He lets himself into my house and kicks off his shoes. "You're going to hate me for this, but…"

I cringe. "Don't say it. Don't."

"We *still* haven't picked a song to sing tonight."

I groan and bump my forehead against the door frame. "I know. I'm supposed to work today but if the shop's quiet I'll ask my mums if I can skip my shift and rehearse instead. Hang on – I need to get dressed."

When I come back downstairs in my uniform, Neon asks if we can take the long route up to the high street to double-check that there aren't any Blanks still wandering around. I don't get the sense that there are any here – Mutti arrived home from the director's house full of ideas about how to fix the plot holes in her next novel, which has to be a good sign – but Neon will feel safer if he can see it for himself.

Fortunately everything in our town seems to be back to normal. It's a bright Saturday morning, the air cold and crisp beneath a clear blue sky. The streets are busy with people heading to the shops or to activities, and none of them look like they could have come from the Realm. We take a walk through the park, now full of joggers and cyclists and kids playing on the swings or slides. As Neon punts a runaway football back to a five-a-side team, something between the trees catches my eye.

"Look!" I grab Neon's sleeve. "The bunny!"

Hopping around in the long grass is the pink rabbit in the white woolly hat, the invisible friend we saw on my street. The little girl who lives across the road is on the swings in the play area. She grips the chains and demands to go higher and higher as her grown-up chats to two women in thick winter coats. The bunny notices Neon and me looking at them and hops forward. Neon takes a few slow steps into the grass and crouches down, his hands on his knees.

"Ready to go, little dude?" he whispers.

The bunny hesitates, its nose twitching nervously, then scurries over to Neon. It takes a long look at the kid on the swings. She's now laughing hysterically at a pug waddling by and doesn't notice.

"It's OK. She's going to be fine." Neon holds out his hand. "I think you'll be happier back where we came from."

The rabbit puts one small paw in Neon's hand. Beneath the hat, its creamy blue eyes close. A moment later, the rabbit vanishes. I glance over at the kid, but she's now busy picking fallen leaves off the asphalt and showing them to the grown-ups. She won't remember the time her imaginary friend came to visit, but then she's so small she may not have even noticed the difference between this version and the one in her head.

"I think that's the last one." Neon stands up and sinks his hands into his pockets. "Just me left."

"You're a real boy now, Pinocchio." I grin. Neon smiles back, but there's a hint of sadness in his voice. "How do you feel about it, really?"

He chews on his lip for a moment before answering. "No regrets. But honestly? Mixed feelings. I'm really happy I can stay, and it feels right. But I keep remembering I won't see my mom or my friends or Cauliflower ever again, and this huge tidal wave of sadness hits. I feel really guilty that I never had the chance to say goodbye or even explain where I was going."

Soon I'm going to have to close the online accounts I set up for Neon's mum and his friends. It'd be way too much work for me to keep them up long-term, and if he wants to live a normal life here, it can't be tangled in so many lies. But, knowing what I now know about the Realm, I suddenly feel horribly guilty too: I've taken him away from Karma and the band, all the friends and relatives I created for him, and without him they're probably going to fade away altogether. But, as we walk past the bakery, an idea comes to me.

"Why don't we write a different ending?" I say. "One where you decide to go back. That way there'll be a second fictional Neon who gets to stay in the Realm."

Neon loves this idea so much, he jumps up into the air and almost knocks over a man leaving the bakery with a macaroni pie. We sit down on a bench, and I take out my phone and open the notes app to write an alternative version of his story: one where Neon stayed here for a week, then went back to his life in the Realm. In that version, Neon tells Karma that he's ready to move on from home-schooling. He applies to a performing-arts high school, the same one that his friends Yifei and Kairo attend, and of course he gets in – he even adds that the judges give him a standing ovation after his audition.

The first time I wrote Neon's story, I tried to keep it mostly realistic. This time, we give the characters what we imagine to be their best possible ending. The Pyramid Club get a record deal and become exactly the right amount of famous: enough that they sell out shows worldwide, but not so much that they can't go out for a meal without being swarmed by fans. Karma marries a painter, and they move to California to set up an art retreat. Cauliflower has three puppies, which the new Neon names Broccoli, Sprout and Bok Choy, and he keeps them all. We give everyone a happily-ever-after. It can't be like that in the real world, but in our story we decide.

By the time we've finished, Neon seems much lighter again. "There. That's the best goodbye I could give them." His lip wobbles for a moment, but he smiles as he stands up. "Time for a new beginning."

"Hey – how about we sing 'Go Your Own Way', the Fleetwood Mac song?" I say, the idea popping up like a light bulb in my head. "I think it's about a break-up, but the title fits your situation."

"I love that song!" Neon gives my arm a faux punch of appreciation. "You're full of good ideas today. The Blanks really must be gone."

We loop back along the high street, which has suddenly become unusually busy. When we pass Every Book & Cranny, I look through the windows to wave to Gio and my mums – then stop in my tracks. The shop is so full of people that I can't even see the desk. Neon and I exchange looks of surprise, then hurry inside, excusing ourselves over and over as we edge towards the till. Gio and Mum are both busy talking to customers, and Mutti is ringing up one of the Nessie colouring books that we've had on the shelves for years while a man and a little girl wait by the counter.

"What's going on?" I ask.

"The videos taken at the loch last night have been picked up by a bunch of news sites." Mutti passes the book to the girl with a smile. "Feels like half the country has come here to try to spot whatever was in the water."

"I'm usually a bit of a cynic about these things, but a couple of experts said the footage seems to be authentic," the man says. "We couldn't see anything this morning, but maybe we'll have more luck after lunch."

"It's *definitely* the Loch Ness Monster," the little girl adds, clutching her colouring book to her chest. "I could see her tail in the video."

The pair move on to let a woman holding three hardbacks get to the front of the line. Joel appears with a stack of colouring books, pushes them into my arms and asks me to display them in the children's section before disappearing back into the stockroom. It feels like we've fast-forwarded to the weeks before Christmas, the only time of year when the shop bustles with customers like this. And, for the second time since my mums told me we had to say goodbye to Every Book & Cranny, I feel another tiny glimmer of hope.

Thirty-five

The shop is still busy when Neon and I arrive back at Every Book & Cranny later that evening. Gio helps us move the tables and sofas around to make room for a small stage and four rows of seats, which fill up in a few minutes. I've never even seen most of the people here, but there are a few familiar faces – Martha from Bohemian Catsody is in the front row, and Mrs Henderson the librarian sits at the back with her husband and kids. Nerves surge through me seeing so many people, but I push them down. Neon and I spent all afternoon practising 'Go Your Own Way' back at Carrie's house and we sounded really good. I'm ready for this.

Caitlin and Hannah are the next performers to turn up. They're already in their dance costumes – hot-pink leotards with lime-green tights and yellow leg warmers – and they have a lot of questions about what went on last night.

"It's so weird... I remember hurrying down to the loch, and I've got this video on my phone," Hannah says, showing me a fuzzy clip of lights moving on the dark water. "But I can't remember filming it. I don't actually remember *seeing* anything, and neither can Caitlin."

"I mean…" Neon looks at me and scratches the back of his head, trying to find an excuse. "Maybe it was the shock? It was definitely a weird night."

"What about the Blanks?" I ask, lowering my voice. "Those people without faces?"

Caitlin's nose wrinkles. "No – you're joking, right? Is that some *Doctor Who* thing?" She rolls her eyes and tugs on her ponytail. "You've been spending too much time with Tilly and her friends."

It turns out Elsie and Jamie don't remember much of what happened last night, either, and nothing about the Blanks that they helped Tilly trap in school while Neon and I ran away. Just like with the cù-sìth, only those of us who know about the Realm are able to remember seeing any of the characters that have disappeared. While Jamie goes over her routine, and Elsie takes a seat beside Hari and Russell, Tilly and I exchange a look and smile. I'm glad that I could share this baffling, weird, amazing experience with her. With Joel and my mums too. Maybe I don't need to keep as many secrets as I thought.

Mr Ross and his band arrive next, followed by Mikey the cellist and Carrie with her theremin, which turns out to be a strange electronic instrument. At half past seven, Mum and Gio squeeze through the crowd to the stage area to announce the start of the show. Mum's wearing her favourite blue satin dress, and Gio's made his moustache extra twirly for the occasion.

"Thank you all so much for coming to Every Book & Cranny's first-ever open-mic night," Gio says, smiling. "As you know, my brilliant co-worker Laurie and her friends have organised this event to try to save us from having to close. Though we've actually got some news about that…"

He turns to Mum. She links her hands together and bounces on the balls of her feet, partly nervous, partly excited. The corners of her mouth twitch from trying not to smile too widely.

"Thanks to a few videos that went viral last night, we've had our best day of sales in three years. So good, in fact, that between that and your generous entrance donations … it looks like we're going to be able to stay open for a few more months." She holds her hands up before anyone gets too excited. "We're not out of the woods yet, but it's a start!"

The audience erupts into applause. I spin round to find Mutti and Joel. They're sitting by the till, both beaming. Neon cups his hands round his mouth and whoops so loudly that a man in the back row winces and covers his ear. My throat gets tight, and I have to blink twenty times to stop myself from crying and ruining my make-up. I don't want to get my hopes up too high, but we don't have to say goodbye to the shop just yet. Right now that's everything.

Neon has offered to be the show's MC, so he squeezes to the front and introduces Caitlin and Hannah as the first act. Their routine is actually brilliant – Hannah even manages to do a full cartwheel across the tiny stage, which gets a huge cheer.

After them comes Jamie. Now that the Blanks aren't around to put her off, her stand-up routine goes perfectly, and she's *hilarious*. She does an impression of her uncles squabbling over the remote control that cracks everyone up.

Next Tilly performs two pieces of poetry. One is called 'Story', about getting lost in other worlds, and the other has the title 'Unicorn', inspired by Aurora. They're both beautiful, and I feel really proud of Tilly for sharing them with everyone. Mikey the cello prodigy plays something by a composer called Shostakovich, which is unsurprisingly excellent, and then Mr Ross's band squeeze in for an acoustic rendition of a Fall Out Boy song.

"And next up we have…" Neon drums his hands on the mic stand while I take long, deep breaths, trying to steady my nerves. "Laurie Storey-Peters!"

I spin round to stare at him. He beams at me, looking like he's invented sliced bread. I shoot a nervous smile at the audience, then take Neon's elbow and lead him away from the mic.

"What are you talking about? You aren't going to sing with me?"

"I'll sing with you after," he says. "I think you should do one on your own first."

"Neon, that wasn't our deal! I can't do it by myself."

"Dude, of course you can! Just sing whatever song comes to mind, and I'll play for you." He puts his hands on my shoulders. "I'm still right here but I want you to see that you don't *need* me, Laurie. You're more than good enough on your own."

Part of me wants to walk out, another part to kill him – but I'm aware that there are almost a hundred people watching us have this conversation, so neither is a good option. With another wobbly smile, I walk up to the microphone. Dozens of faces look back at me. Mum and Mutti smile. Joel gives me a double thumbs up and looks like a total dork. Every cell in my body is screaming at me to get out of there, and it takes everything in me not to spin round and sprint through the door.

But then I close my eyes, and I think about the past two weeks. I think about the fact that I got onstage at Friday Showcase and at least *tried*, something I would never have done before. I remember facing the cù-sìth, how I didn't run and leave Neon on his own, even though I was terrified. I remember standing in front of the final Blank and telling Neon's story, even though it could have wiped away my imagination like condensation on glass. Neon has saved me in so many ways, but I saved him too.

He's right. I *can* do this.

I open my eyes and find the audience still there, waiting patiently. Everyone is here to help the shop. No one is going to laugh if I mess up. No one is hoping that I fail. They're just waiting to hear a song.

Turning to Neon, I nod. He grins back, another reminder that he's here for me, that I've got this. So I open my mouth, and I sing. I sing the first song that comes into my head, without questioning if it's the right choice, without worrying if I'm going to mess up or forget the lyrics halfway through. I sing the way I do in my room at home, my voice bright and loud and clear. I sing, and I let myself be heard.

Acknowledgements

Publishing a book is very much a team effort,
and I'm lucky to get to work with such great people
on mine. Thank you to the entire Little Tiger team,
particularly my editors Mattie Whitehead and Karelle
Tobias for their expert guidance in shaping
Neon and Laurie's story.

Thank you to Pip Johnson for designing
another wonderful cover, and to Helder Oliveira
for illustrating it so beautifully!

Thank you to Dan Shapiro, Linda Freund,
Andrew Critchley and Grace Kavanagh for their
valuable feedback on early drafts.

Thank you as always to my friends and family
for their support, especially to Naïa for helping me find
the time to write in between work and our sons' many
social engagements!

Finally, I like to think of *A Flash of Neon*
as a little homage to stories in all their many forms, so
thank you to the people who do such essential work
in sharing stories with those around them: librarians,
teachers, booksellers, reviewers, storytellers of all kinds.
This one is for you!

"A beautiful exploration of grief, hope, and what it means
to be human. This is an outstanding middle-grade debut from
one of my favourite authors."
Simon James Green, author of *Finn Jones Was Here*

On a small island off the Scottish coast, Isla and her family are grieving
the loss of her older sister Flora, who died three years ago. Then they're
offered the chance to be part of a top-secret trial, which revives loved
ones as fully lifelike AI robots using their digital footprint.

Isla has her doubts about Second Chances, but they evaporate
the moment the 'new' Flora arrives. This girl is not some uncanny close
likeness; she is Flora – a perfect replica. But not everyone on their island
feels the same. And as the threats to Flora mount, she grows distant
and more secretive. Will Isla be able to protect the new Flora
and bring the community back together?

"An intriguing and tender portrayal of a life changing 'what if'
– Sophie Cameron is a fabulous storyteller."
Polly Ho-Yen, author of *Boy in the Tower*

"A page-turning book about finding your place and your voice, it's about the power and the pain and the colour of language too. I loved it."
Perdita Cargill, author of *Diary of an Accidental Witch*

Set in a world where words appear physically when people speak, *Away With Words* explores the importance of communication and being there for those we love.

Gala and her dad Jordi have just moved from home in Cataluña to a town in Scotland, to live with Jordi's boyfriend Ryan. Gala doesn't speak much English, and feels lost, lonely and unable to be her usual funny self.

Until she befriends Natalie, a girl with selective mutism. The two girls find their own ways to communicate, which includes collecting other people's discarded words. They use the words to write anonymous supportive poems for their classmates, but then someone begins leaving nasty messages using the same method – and the girls are blamed. Gala has finally started adapting to her new life in Scotland and is determined to find the culprit. Can she and Natalie show the school who they really are?

"Brave, clever, and innovative … demonstrates the very best of what children's fiction can do – it's pure, lyrical magic from start to finish."
Zoe Markham, Netgalley

Read on for an extract from:

Away With Words

One

The head teacher had *slugs* on his face. Lime–green, right in the middle of his chin.

Not the animal – the word.

The word *slugs* stuck to his chin in lime-green letters.

"Welcome ～～～, Gala," Mr Watson said. "～～～～～ school."

At least, that was how it sounded to me. I tried to read the missing words as they fell from the head teacher's mouth – they were bright and bold, egg-yolk yellow – but I was too distracted by the *slugs* on his face. Why had he been talking about slugs so early in the morning? Maybe he was a gardener and was worried about his vegetables. Maybe he stepped on one on his way into school and felt bad about it. Maybe he'd eaten them for breakfast. Maybe that was normal in Scotland.

Mr Watson must have noticed me staring because he brushed his hand over his chin, and the word *slugs* fell on to the desk. "I think you ～～～ ～～～," he told me. "～～～～～ change, but ～～～～."

The sentence dropped

piece

by

piece

from Mr Watson's mouth and disappeared into the pile of words in front of him. It wasn't even nine o'clock yet, and his desk already looked like he'd spat out half a dictionary! I saw a few words I knew — a small grey *cold* caught behind the space bar on the keyboard, *music* in cursive purple letters by his coffee cup — but I still had no clue what he was saying.

Beside me, Papa smiled and nodded. "Gala is very ～～～ ～～～," he said, putting his hand on my shoulder. His voice slipped into that funny up-and-down thing it always did when he spoke English, as if his vocal cords were riding a carousel. "I am sure ～～～ ～～～ happy here."

The word *happy* caught on the collar of Papa's jacket. It was a light blue lie. I wasn't happy to be here. I didn't want to be in Scotland at all. It had only been five days since we'd moved here from Cadaqués, a little town by the sea in the north-east of Spain, but I already missed it so much it hurt. I wanted to be back at my old school, racing my friend Pau down the corridor and getting into trouble for talking too much in class. I wanted to go home.

As words spilled from the head teacher's mouth, there was a knock on the door. Mr Watson said a large orange, "Yes?", and two girls stepped into the office. They were both around my age, almost twelve. One was White and very tall with freckles and light brown hair, and the other was Black and short with smiley brown eyes and braces on her teeth. The tall one said something, and Mr Watson nodded.

"Thank you, ～～～. Gala, this is ～～～ and ～～～～," he said, turning back to me. "They ～～～."

The girls smiled awkwardly at me as Mr Watson talked. There was a word he kept saying, something I'd never heard before. I realized from the way he was pointing to the girls that it was a name. When Papa nudged me to reply, I quickly scanned the desk and found it dangling from the tip of a pencil in Mr Watson's pen pot: *Eilidh.*

"Hello –" I tried to sound out the word – "Eyelid?"

The girls blinked at me, then the tall one's eyes went wide, and she said a lot of bright pink words very, very quickly.

Seeing I was lost, Papa finally switched to Catalan, the language we spoke at home. It turned out *Eilidh* was their name – both of them, Eilidh Chisholm and Eilidh Obiaka – and it was pronounced 'A-lee'.

Mr Watson and Papa both chuckled at my mistake, and the girls giggled too. It wasn't a mean sort of laughter, but I felt my cheeks go red. Why bother spelling it E-I-L-I-D-H if they weren't going to pronounce half the letters? That made no sense whatsoever.

Outside Mr Watson's office, a bell rang. He and Papa stood up and moved towards the door, so I did the same. From the way the Eilidhs lingered by the doorway, I guessed they were here to show me to my first class. The one with braces, Eilidh O, gave me another smile and stepped aside to let me into the corridor.

It was noisy now, dozens of kids laughing or swinging their bags or shoving last-minute breakfasts into their mouths as they went to their classes. This place was bigger than my last school, and with everyone rushing around it felt enormous – there must have been twice as many kids here. But that wasn't the reason my mouth fell open.

It was because of the words.

Hundreds and thousands of words falling out of mouths

and flying through the air,

bouncing off

walls

and

fluttering

to

the

floor.

ANGRY RED WORDS and happy yellow ones. *Timid whispers in pastel tones* and **excited shouts in bold, thick fonts**. There were tired words that **blurred with a yawn around the edges**, and *sleek cursive words that could only have come from rumours and secrets*. There were so many that they already came up past my ankles – a glittering stream of speech curving past the reception desk and along the corridor as kids splashed through it without a second thought.

My old school was filled with words too. Back there, I never paid them much attention. Sometimes my friends and I would flick them across the desk to each other when we were bored in class, but I'd never thought about how many there were around us. Not even when the school cleaners came to sweep them all away at the end of the day. When I was speaking Catalan or Spanish, I hardly noticed when the words left my mouth – I just brushed them off my clothes or picked them away if they landed in my food. Here they were all I could see, all I could hear. And I could barely understand anything.

About the Author

Sophie Cameron is a YA and MG author from the Scottish Highlands. Her debut MG novel *Our Sister, Again* won the Leeds Book Awards, and *Away With Words* was shortlisted for the Carnegie Medal for Writing, UKLA Award, Polari Prize, Spark! Book Awards, and a runner-up at the Diverse Book Awards. She lives in Spain with her family.